DECISIVE MEASURES

Helicopter pilot Jack Griffiths arrives in war-torn Sierra Leone to take up a job transporting supplies and personnel to a Western-owned diamond mine. A respite, he hopes, from his recent, horrific experience of military combat.

But, in the torrid heat of Africa Jack finds himself involved, yet again, in fierce fighting. And among those he has to protect is Layla, a beautiful local doctor to whom he is powerfully drawn.

DECISIVE MEASURES

SELECT EDITIONS

This condensation has been created by The Reader's Digest Association Limited by special arrangement with Hodder Headline plc.

With the exception of actual personages identified as such, the characters and incidents in this volume are entirely the products of the author's imagination and have no relation to any person or events in real life.

The original edition of this book was published and copyrighted as follows: DECISIVE MEASURES, published at £16.99 by Hodder and Stoughton, © 2000 by John Nichol. Author photo on page 143 © Stephen Gill. The right of John Nichol to be identified as the author of this work has been asserted by him in accordance with the Copyright, Designs and Patents Act 1988. Cover images and front cover/spine of slipcase photomontage (second from right): helicopter: Quadrant Picture Library; man's face: Superstock; photomontage by John Calvert. Slipcase photomontage by Shark Attack.

The Reader's Digest Association Limited,
11 Westferry Circus, Canary Wharf, London E14 4HE.

www.readersdigest.co.uk
ISBN 0 276 42552 9

Printed and bound by GGP Media, Pössneck, Germany

JOHN NICHOL

DECISIVE MEASURES

READER'S DIGEST SELECT EDITIONS
CONDENSED BOOKS DIVISION

PROLOGUE

The sunset was already reddening the sky and casting long shadows across the hills when the radio crackled into life again. ‘Echo Fourteen. Hostiles reported 179502. Investigate.’

I suppressed a groan and acknowledged the order. We had been flying for over eight hours, sortie after sortie over a land already scarred by fighting, arriving always too late, to find another village in ruins, another pillar of black smoke reaching up into the sky.

I banked the heli around and headed northeast over the dusty Macedonian hills. I dropped to low level as we approached the Kosovan border, and began twisting and turning, hugging the contours of the land. We soared to clear a last mountain ridge and then dropped into the target valley.

Ahead was a familiar scene: a hamlet, a cluster of houses sheltering in the lee of the hills, surrounded by a belt of woodland. I could see columns of smoke and the flicker of flames piercing the jagged outlines of ruined houses. Of the inhabitants there was no sign.

I put the heli into a broad turn around the hamlet, my eyes raking the open ground and the edges of the woodland. Out of the corner of my eye, I glimpsed a group of rectilinear outlines in the shadows among the trees—trucks or maybe even tanks using the wood for cover. My flesh crept, but I maintained the same course until we had passed out of sight beyond the end of the wood. I radioed base. ‘Possible hostiles sighted. Over.’

Then I jabbed the intercom. 'Keep alert, guys. There are at least six vehicles among the trees. I'm making another pass along the edge of the wood. Echo Thirteen, follow me through.'

I heard a thud behind me as the gunner slid open the door of the cab and swung his gun to cover the target. I swooped in low and fast past the edge of the wood, using my peripheral vision to search for the outlines among the trees. Once more there was no sign of people and no firing, only the tantalising, half-hidden shapes.

I had now made out eight distinct forms under the trees and a long, tapering black cylinder angled upwards at 45 degrees. It could have been the barrel of a tank gun; it could equally have been a fallen tree. I passed beyond the end of the wood and banked in a tight turn, as my wingman followed me through. The intercom crackled as he completed his pass. 'Definite hostiles,' he said. 'Let's go for it.'

I hesitated. 'Negative. Am not sure. Going in again.'

As we dropped back towards the wood, I lowered our speed. A flash of the dying sunlight reflected from my copilot's helmet as he turned to look at me. 'Jesus, Jack,' he said. 'How much of an invitation are you going to give them?'

'We've got to be sure.'

'We'll be sure enough when we're dead.'

As we reached the midpoint of the wood, I flared the heli, putting it into the hover. The force of the downwash threw the branches aside for a moment and I at last saw movement—figures sprinting towards the vehicles. I sped up and away from the wood.

I reached for the radio. 'Figures and vehicles sighted.'

The answer came back before I had posed the question. 'Clear engage.'

I kept circling. My wingman's voice came over the intercom. 'What are we waiting for?'

My copilot's gaze was still fixed on me. 'Well?' he said.

Abruptly I made the decision. 'Engage.'

I headed out in a wide loop and then dropped to minimum level, accelerating back towards the long shadow of the wood. The trees rose like a dark wall ahead of us. I held the heli level for a few more seconds as I stared into the cross hairs. They intersected on the largest shape inside the trees and I pulled the trigger once, twice.

There was a *whoosh* as the rockets streaked from the pod. I sent the heli soaring up into the sky. A moment later, there was a massive explosion and a bubble of oily flame and black smoke belched upwards through the trees. The gun thundered as the door gunner raked the edge of the wood. There was no answering fire.

I saw my wingman complete his attack run as I banked for another pass. I dropped in low, the turbines screaming, my finger once more tightening on the trigger. A microsecond before I fired, a figure burst from the wood, a human torch burning from head to toe. The long black skirt flapping around the woman's legs was a sheet of flame.

I jabbed the intercom button. 'Abort. Abort.' I peered down. The woman was still wreathed in flame, her arms raised, her hands spread wide in supplication. She threw her head back. I saw her mouth opening in a silent scream. Then she slumped to the ground, a shapeless, burning mound of rags.

I turned for base, the ground blurring before my eyes as tears trickled down my face.

CHAPTER 1

A wall of heat and humidity hit us as the door of the aircraft swung open. Sweat beaded my forehead at once as I watched two Africans in threadbare overalls push a rusting flight of steps to the plane.

Tom leaned past me and stared out at the airfield. From his expression he was less than impressed. Over forty years old, and a career RAF man, he was finding it hard to adjust to life on the outside. 'That must be the welcoming committee,' he said, as a cloud of flies formed around us.

'Welcome to the real world, Tom. Better get used to it. There's no more soft postings and squadron dinners for us, and no more people to hold our hands and tidy up after us. We're on our own now.'

He scowled and the ever-present frown lines deepened on his

forehead. 'What a dump. Remind me what we're doing here, Jack.'

'We're doing the only job we know, making a few quid for ourselves and upholding Her Majesty's vital interests at the same time.'

He gave a sour smile. 'Vital interests spelt D-I-A-M-O-N-D-S. If they're that vital, why doesn't Her Majesty send some of her own boys to look after them? No, don't tell me, let me guess: because some things are better done at arm's length.'

I met his gaze. 'Listen, it's a job of work. We agreed to the terms when we signed the contract. It's a bit late now for regrets.'

We hurried down the steps and walked across the potholed concrete towards the terminal building. It was stained and crumbling and its windows were filthy and starred with bullet holes.

Tom's thinning, sandy hair was darkened and plastered to his head by sweat. I could feel my shirt sticking to my back.

Although the shedlike arrivals hall was out of the sun, it felt little cooler. Two soldiers in grease-stained uniforms got up as we approached. They pored over our passports, then dropped them onto the table in front of them. We waited in silence, searching their impassive faces for some clue to the next move.

A group of African men, women and children, most in torn clothes and ragged T-shirts, stood on the far side of the steel gates beyond the arrivals hall, staring at us without apparent interest. There was a commotion and the group parted to allow two men through. They opened the gates and came striding towards us.

The leader was a powerful figure, his skin tanned to mahogany from long exposure to the sun and his hair flecked with grey. A broad grin showed beneath his walrus moustache. Ignoring the soldiers, he walked over and slapped us on the back. 'Glad you made it, boys. Grizz Riley. You can't imagine how pleased I am to see you here. I was beginning to think we'd never get another heli crew.'

As he spoke, his companion, a paunchy African with a gold tooth and a shiny suit, began talking to the soldiers in confidential tones. I recognised the type, a local fixer paid to smooth our way past police, customs and other local piranhas.

I heard the words 'Decisive Measures', and the rustle of leone bills—the local currency. Pocketing the bribe, the two soldiers, now all smiles, handed us back our passports and waved us through.

Grizz led us outside to a battered pick-up. A bullet-headed, square-jawed soldier in faded fatigues stood guard over it. His blond hair was cropped so short that his scalp showed through it, and a network of scar lines gleamed white against the tanned skin. He remained unsmiling, scrutinising each of us in turn.

'Another new kid on the block,' Grizz said.

'Jack Griffiths,' I said, holding out my hand. 'Pleased to meet you.'

The soldier scowled, but shook my hand. 'I'm Rudi,' he said in a thick Afrikaans accent.

Rudi and the fixer got in the front while we climbed into the back with Grizz. A few heads turned to watch us drive off.

It was an uncomfortable ride. The airport road was potholed and badly scarred by tank tracks. The rusting, burnt-out wreck of one tank had been bulldozed off the road and then left to rot.

We reached the main road that led up the peninsula towards Freetown. Its surface was marginally better and we accelerated towards the capital. The sun was now directly overhead and I was glad of the patches of dappled shade as the road weaved through fringes of rain forest. At intervals there were clusters of mud-and-thatch huts, and an occasional concrete building. Signs advertised bars, shops and cafés, but all appeared to be closed, and many were smoke-blackened and pockmarked by gunfire.

We climbed a forested ridge and saw Freetown sprawling below us, a mosaic of bare earth, grey concrete, palm thatch and multi-coloured tin roofing, all overlaid with a layer of red dust.

Beyond the capital, palm-fringed, white-sand beaches, stretching south along the peninsula as far as I could see, looked deserted. This was clearly no place for tourists. Commanding the ridge line were rows of colonial houses raised above the earth on stilts and shaded by breadfruit and cotton trees. Grizz followed my gaze. 'It was named Hill Station by the British,' he said.

Like their former occupants, the houses had once been white, but they were now faded to a dull khaki brown, stained by rivulets of damp. All of them were surrounded by high brick walls or tin fences topped with shards of broken glass and coils of razor wire.

Mango and breadfruit trees grew in the lush grounds of the Presidential Palace on Signal Hill, but the white walls, unrepaired from years of coups and countercoups, were pitted by shellfire. Lower on the steep hillside the slopes festered with an ugly, sprawling shantytown that ran down to the creek at the bottom of the hill. The shacks were built of packing cases and scrap wood, and roofed with rusting corrugated metal or palm fronds.

Ahead of us, a few overloaded, battered pick-ups drove down the hill into the city, laden with firewood and farm goods to sell. As we rounded a bend on the steep descent, we came to a juddering halt. A pick-up and a beaten-up old Mercedes taxi had collided. Both drivers were out of their vehicles, remonstrating with each other.

As they argued, a human tide began pouring out of the shantytown on the hillside just below the road. Ignoring the drivers' protests and tearful pleas, the mob began looting the vehicles, stripping them of everything they could carry. The Mercedes driver tried to save his car radio, but he was punched to the ground.

Drivers coming up the hill stopped, sized up the situation and either reversed or pulled three-point turns and disappeared in clouds of dust. A moment later a police car appeared round the corner. It braked to a halt and sounded its siren. The looters barely glanced up from their work of stripping the cars. No policemen emerged from the car and after a moment it, too, reversed down the hill.

Grizz glanced at me. 'Welcome to Sierra Leone,' he said. He reached for his rifle, stood up and fired a burst into the air. Then he lowered the barrel, pointing it at the looters. There was a moment's silence, then they fled in panic and we drove on into the city.

At the Kissy roundabout we turned west through the Lebanese district and drove down East Street past the mosque and the prison. The decaying façades of once-imposing colonial buildings lined the broad streets at the centre of Freetown, but City Hall was a crumbling wreck, surrounded by rows of shabby two-storey buildings. Tattered washing hung from lines suspended across the street, and most of the houses had a fire pit in the yard in place of a kitchen.

We pulled up in Garrison Street by a row of battered shops with buckled and scorched steel shutters. Most were run by Lebanese traders, but few had any goods to offer; only a handful of tins and flyblown packages on otherwise empty shelves.

The general store at the end of the street was slightly better equipped, though the goods seemed more appropriate to a frontier town than a capital city. There were mosquito nets, candles, axes, bush knives and the shovels and sieves used by gold panners.

Grizz busied himself collecting supplies, which Rudi took out and loaded onto the pick-up, while the store owner ran around scribbling notes on a pad. We left the fixer to argue about the price, and Grizz led us round the corner to a hotel. It resembled a Soviet apartment block and had perversely been built back to front. The balconies faced inland and the bathrooms looked out over the sea.

Grizz left us at the check-in desk.

'When do we start work?' I said.

He smiled. 'Decisive Measures are generous employers. You get one night's acclimatisation and R 'n' R. Then we go upcountry to the Bohara mine first thing in the morning. I'll leave you guys to sort your kit. I'll be back at six to give you a briefing and then show you what passes for a good time in these parts.' He sauntered out.

My room was everything I expected: the lights didn't work, nor did the rusting fan at the centre of the bedroom ceiling. There was a rustle of cockroaches from the bathroom and a stench that made me reluctant to investigate further.

A kerosene lamp stood by the bed, which was draped with a mosquito net. I turned back the covers, lay down and closed my eyes.

I woke soaked with sweat, my heart pounding, the thunder of gunfire still resounding in my ears. Only the noise of the cicadas broke the silence of my room. As I lowered my head back to the pillow, cursing the nightmare that had frightened me awake, I heard the banging of fists on the door and Grizz's voice shouting, 'Come on, you lazy bastard. I've nearly worn my knuckles off on this door.'

I croaked a reply.

'Twenty minutes, in the lobby,' he said.

When I heard his footsteps recede down the corridor, I dragged myself out of bed and walked into the bathroom.

I turned on the shower and stood under the dribble of brackish water for a few minutes, then towelled myself dry. I pulled on jeans and a clean long-sleeved shirt, then headed down the stairs, not wishing to try my luck with the lift.

I found Grizz, Rudi and Tom in the lobby, staring out through the plate-glass window at the skyline. There had been a slow build-up of cloud throughout the afternoon, climbing the wall of the mountains and piling higher and higher into the sky, building the thunderheads that would bring the evening rain. The sun had almost set and lightning was sparking over the mountains.

As the sky darkened, the lights all over Freetown went out. Tom started and looked round in alarm. 'Just another power failure,' Grizz said. For a moment the city was in darkness, then scores of generators fired up in a metallic chorus, counterpointing the croaking of the frogs in the swamps.

We walked to a small meeting room off the lobby. Marks of smoke damage and the crudely repaired outline of an impact from a heavy round or rocket were clearly visible where the wall met the ceiling.

We settled into chairs as Grizz closed the door. He strode to the front of the room. 'Rudi, you can sleep through the first bit if you want, unless helicopter-spotting is one of your hobbies.'

He turned to Tom and me. 'Have you guys flown together before?'

'You mean apart from the training course on the Huey?' I said. 'Not for a while. Tom trained me though, nearly ten years ago.'

'It won't be a problem,' Tom said. 'We both know our own jobs.'

Grizz nodded. 'OK, as I'm sure you've been told, you'll be flying a Huey XI. The helicopter is vital to the resupply and support of the garrison at the Bohara mine. You'll be based here in Freetown, but your job is to keep Bohara supplied with everything from mining equipment and ammunition to food and medical supplies. The Huey is twenty years old, but it's been upgraded many times and I can vouch for its condition. It has a door-mounted mini-gun, a nose gun and forward-firing rockets, and chaff and flare dispensers. It's also been fitted out for flight with night-vision goggles.'

'What about the rebels?' Tom said. 'What have they got?'

Rudi stirred and began to show some interest.

'They're backed by Liberia,' Grizz said, 'and a lot of their weapons come through that regime. They have plenty of AK rifles, a few rocket-propelled grenades and a couple of heavy machine guns. They also captured a ZFU antiaircraft gun from the government some years ago, but we're uncertain whether they have the know-how to fire it effectively. The Liberians do have Hind helicopters, however, and there are rumours that one has been allocated to the rebels. You'll have read about Sierra Leone in the papers, but in some ways the reality here surpasses anything you've heard. The government is theoretically in control of the country, but in practice its writ barely runs as far as the outskirts of Freetown.'

He gave a bleak smile. 'Lives have no value here. Only one thing counts: diamonds. The government owns the mines but is powerless to protect them without the help of private military companies like Decisive Measures, and, like everybody else, the companies take their reward in gemstones. Don't get the idea that we operate on a lavish budget though, we operate on a shoestring.'

'What are the rebels fighting for?' I said.

Grizz shrugged. 'Just diamonds. They want to defeat the government, but only so they can take control of the diamond-producing areas. The rebels are bloody and brutal fighters but they're not particularly well equipped; the Liberian regime that backs them creams off most of the diamond wealth that the rebels steal or smuggle out.

'The regular army is supposed to be on our side but, despite the diamonds, this is the poorest country in the world and the soldiers certainly aren't growing too fat for their uniforms. When they're paid at all it's sporadic, and they're going hungry: they're supposed to get one bag of rice a month plus clothing and a gun, but the senior officers keep back as much rice as they can to sell on the black market.

'In short, we can rely on no one but ourselves here. If it all goes to ratshit, the British government and the UN won't want to know. There will be no SAS rescue parties flying in to save our arses. We either look after ourselves or we go under.'

He paused. 'That's the bad news; the good news is that for the moment we're in a lull in the fighting. The rebel offensive in the northeast has stalled because of the rainy season. With the dry season almost upon us we must expect an upsurge in activity. For the moment, though, Decisive Measures are simply tasked with keeping the Bohara diamond mine running smoothly. Your job is to get the supplies and the personnel out there to enable it to do so. That's it. Any questions? Then let's go and have a beer.'

WE WENT OUT into the hot, humid night. It was low tide and the sickly, fetid smell of mud and mangroves filled the air.

Women sat at the side of the street, their goods—dried fish, rice, cassava roots, chillies and potato leaf—spread in front of them on palm leaves laid in the dust. Their hungry, pot-bellied children played around them as they waited.

Here and there a solitary streetlight flickered into life as the power was restored, but most were broken, their wiring stolen and sold for scrap, or cannibalised for other uses.

We passed several burnt-out and derelict houses. Those that remained intact had iron-barred windows, stout locks and razor-wire fences. The walls were still clapboard, however.

Grizz led us along the road fringing the beach. It was lined with restaurants. From the nameboards over the doors, most of them, like the shops, were run by Lebanese. Many were deserted, but at one the owner still presided over his bamboo-fronted bar, perched on a rusting stool, his paunch spilling out of his torn, stained T-shirt. The bar was full of expatriate mineworkers, traders, soldiers and government officials, and a scattering of dull-eyed whores.

The menu was limited: groundnut soup and rice. I ordered food and beer for all four of us.

Grizz took a swig of his beer, lit a cheroot and glanced at Tom. 'So what brings you here, Tom? Apart from the money, of course. Bottom line, that's what we're all here for, isn't it?'

Tom sipped his drink. 'Money and boredom, I suppose,' he said. 'I've been pensioned off by the RAF, but it's a bit early in my life to be getting out the pipe and slippers, so I thought I'd give this a go.'

'Any family?'

'No. Well, I've two children, but they're grown-up now. One lives in Australia and the other's in New York.'

'And your wife's back in England?'

As Tom stared down into his beer, the overhead light deepened the furrows in his forehead and he looked even older than his forty-five years. 'She left me a few months ago.'

Grizz studied him for a moment. 'So your break-up would have been another reason for a change of scene?'

Tom didn't reply. After a moment, Grizz switched his attention to me. 'What about you, Jack? You're too young to have been pensioned off. What's the story? Rub some air marshal up the wrong way?'

'Something like that.'

Grizz waited for me to continue. As the silence lengthened, he smiled. 'Fair enough. It's none of my business, anyway, as long as you do your job here.' He shot a glance at Rudi. 'And you're certainly not the only one working for Decisive Measures who's got a bit of a history behind him.' He paused. 'So . . . got any wives or children?'

'Not last time I looked,' I said. 'What about you?'

'Plenty of each—three wives, four children. All in the past tense now, though.'

'Even the children?'

'Oh, I send them a card on their birthdays and things, but it only upsets them if I go to see them. It's better all round if I stay away.' He tried to force a smile, but his eyes belied it.

'And you, Rudi?' I said.

'Fifteen years in the South African Defence Force fighting bush wars against the ANC. I quit the day Mandela was sworn in.'

'Any family?'

He shook his head and ended the interrogation by walking over to the bar. By the time he returned with more beer, Tom, Grizz and I had moved the conversation on to less personal ground.

Rudi stayed aloof from the chat, downing a succession of beers and replying in monosyllables to any remarks directed at him, but his watchful eyes showed that he missed little of what was said. Finally, as if we had passed some secret test, he banged another four beers down on the table and gave a broad smile. He took a long pull on his drink, then put his feet up on the table and rocked his chair back.

'This could be God's country, Jack—perfect beaches, diamonds, any woman you want for the price of a pack of cigarettes, and just enough trouble from the rebels to keep us in work. You couldn't have a better posting.' His speech was a little slurred, and though he smiled he had the air of a man who could change moods in a second.

As Rudi was warming to his theme, a taxi pulled up outside. A few moments later two tall, striking women entered the bar. One had long black hair cascading around her powerful shoulders, a mouth lipsticked in vivid red and skin so dark it seemed blue-black in the dim light. The other was model-thin with close-cropped dark brown hair, coffee-coloured skin and eyes of piercing blue. I could not take my eyes off her.

'Jesus,' Rudi said. 'Some good-looking whores at last.'

He had just reached the two women when Grizz returned from the bar with another round. He took in the scene and winked at us. 'This should be entertaining.'

Rudi's bulky figure loomed over the two women as he propositioned them, waving a ten-dollar bill. The black woman ignored him, turning her back and talking to the barman. The other heard Rudi out in silence, eyeballing him without blinking. Then she took the bill, tore it in quarters and dropped it on the floor.

'Even if I was a whore,' I heard her say, 'it would take more than you could earn in a lifetime to persuade me to sleep with an ox like you. But I'm not a whore, I'm a paramedic. Part of my job is to patch up dumb mercenaries when they get shot. I look forward to making your acquaintance again under those circumstances.'

Rudi stared at her, the veins knotting in his forehead. I was afraid he might strike her, but he shambled back across the room.

He swore in Afrikaans. 'That bitch needs teaching a lesson.'

Grizz raised an eyebrow. 'That bitch is a bloody good medic. Now have a drink and take your beating like a man. There's plenty of whores will take your money without hitting on women who won't.'

Rudi reverted to sullen silence.

'So who is she?' I asked Grizz.

'She's called Layla. She works for Medicaid International, but she's seconded to us part of the time. She deals with medical problems at the mining compound and holds clinics in the villages.' Grizz smiled. 'And don't waste your time; we've all tried.'

I saw her move to the bar. 'I'll get the next ones,' I said.

I walked over and stood next to her as I ordered the beers, then glanced at her. 'Hi, I'm Jack,' I said. 'I fly helicopters. I gather we'll be working together now and again.'

She looked me up and down. 'I'm Layla.' Her accent was English but with a faint lilt. 'I don't think so. I work with mercenaries as little as possible. My job's to save lives.'

'So's mine.'

'Sure,' she said. 'Just like your friends over there.' She walked back to her table, leaving me staring after her.

I went back to the others. Rudi was still mechanically downing one beer after another and his mood was turning increasingly ugly.

Grizz glanced at him and then at us. 'Maybe we could round the evening off with a couple of beers back at the hotel,' he said.

Rudi shook his head, his eyes still fixed on Layla and her friend. 'Not me. I'll see you later.'

Grizz shrugged. 'You guys with me? I'll just hit the can and we'll be out of here.'

On his way back from the stinking lean-to that acted as the communal toilet, I saw him stop and speak to Layla. She turned and looked at Rudi, then frowned and nodded.

Grizz walked back over to us. 'Let's go.'

Tom and I followed him outside. The taxi that had brought Layla and her friend was still waiting, parked a few yards away. Grizz signalled to it and we climbed in.

'Wait a moment, please,' Grizz said.

Tom looked puzzled. 'What for? Rudi said he was staying put.'

He smiled. 'I think you'll enjoy this company more than Rudi's.'

As we waited, the rain began to fall. In seconds it was battering down, blanking out the view and turning the brown water coursing down the road to foam.

Layla and her friend appeared in the doorway of the bar. They hesitated at the sight of the rain, then glanced behind them and ran for the taxi. By the time they had reached it they were soaked to the skin, their hair plastered to their scalps.

Layla jumped in next to me, her wet clothes clinging to her, showing every contour of her body. As her friend also squeezed onto the crowded back seat, Layla was pressed against me. My nostrils were full of the musky aroma of her perfume, and I could feel the soft swelling of her breast against my arm. The heat of her body seemed to burn all the way down my side.

The taxi moved off along the road, inching through the flood. I glanced behind us. The huge figure of Rudi was visible for a second, framed in the doorway of the bar, staring after us, then the curtains of rain blocked him from view.

We were halfway back to the hotel when the storm ended as abruptly as it had begun. The floods began to ebb away and a watery moon appeared as the clouds parted. Even this late, traders came out of the buildings and doorways where they had been sheltering and began setting up again, lighting candles and storm lanterns to illuminate their wares.

The hotel bar was deserted but still open. 'Fancy a last drink?' I said, unsuccessfully trying to hide my disappointment when Layla exchanged a glance with her friend, then shook her head.

'Nothing personal. We've all got an early start in the morning.'

'Have we?'

'You guys are the helicopter pilots, aren't you?'

'Yes, but—'

'Then don't stay up all night drinking. I'm flying up to Bohara with you in the morning to run a clinic at the mine.' For the first time all evening, she gave me a smile. I could still smell a faint trace of her perfume in the air long after she had disappeared up the stairs.

CHAPTER 2

We set off early the next morning. Layla rode up front with Grizz. Tom and I were once more perched in the back, with Rudi.

The glass had been knocked out of the small window in the rear of the cab, allowing us to talk to Grizz and Layla, though we had to shout to be heard above the roar of the engine.

When we reached the Kissy roundabout, Grizz continued straight on. 'This isn't the way to the airport,' I shouted.

'I know. That's because the helicopter isn't kept there.'

We passed through the belt of dismal shantytowns surrounding the capital, the smoke from cooking fires mingling with the stink of refuse and decay, ragged people moving among the shacks. 'Every rebel offensive sends a few more thousand fleeing to Freetown,' Layla said. 'They all end up in the shantytowns.'

The road ran out into open country along fringes of dense jungle and swamp, and the tarmac gave way to red earth and crushed rock as the road climbed steadily towards the mountains. Looking back I could pick out the huge cotton tree in the centre of Freetown.

We drove on, the surface of the road potholed and fissured by rainwater and floods. Ahead I saw savannah grassland. It looked fertile, studded with breadfruit, pawpaw, guava, mango and locust trees, but the villages were few and sparsely populated.

The road curved to the left and, as we reached the bend, Grizz hit the brakes hard. A tangle of branches had been thrown across the road. Beyond it stood a row of armed men.

I reached down to the rifle beneath my feet. Rudi already had his across his lap, and I heard a click as he eased off the safety catch. There was no way of telling whether the men were soldiers or rebels, since all wore the same battered uniforms, topped with whatever lurid T-shirts or other clothes they had managed to loot. They stood in silence, fingering their weapons and gazing at us with hostility.

'I think they're government men,' Grizz said out of the corner of his mouth. 'Not that it makes much difference. They're hungry and they haven't been paid. That's enough to make anyone bad tempered. Give them some smokes.'

I reached for one of the packs of American cigarettes stashed in the back and held it out over the side of the pick-up as Grizz drove slowly to the makeshift barrier. The leader of the soldiers stepped forward and took the cigarettes. He remained unsmiling, but after a few moments he nodded and signalled his men to move the barrier.

As we moved off, Rudi kept his rifle trained on the group of men, swinging himself slowly round as we nosed through the narrow gap in the barrier, until he was facing back over the tailgate.

We left the road for a rutted dirt track leading away through the bush. It doglegged right and left, and as we swung round the second bend I saw a stretch of rusty wire fencing and a pair of open double gates. The legend on the peeling signboards was just about legible: SIERRA LEONE DEFENCE FORCES, CAMP 17.

Beyond the fence was an expanse of beaten earth and concrete. The barrack huts ahead were so ruinous it seemed inconceivable that the base could still be in use, but a squat soldier appeared from the guardhouse and pointed a Kalashnikov in our direction. His scowl changed to a smile as he recognised Grizz, and he saluted.

Grizz returned the salute and I tossed the soldier a pack of cigarettes as we bounced and jolted our way across the base. We rounded a barrack block and came to a halt by an old Huey parked on the concrete. Even through the camouflage net covering it, I could see it was riddled with holes.

'We're not flying that,' I said. 'Are we? It looks like a wreck.'

Grizz smiled. 'It is. The one you're flying is inside the hangar.' He pointed towards an arch of corrugated-tin sheeting walled with mud bricks. A soldier dozing by the doors leapt to attention and was rewarded with another pack of cigarettes.

Grizz kicked at the rotting wooden doors to loosen them, then we dragged them open. 'Same model,' he said, 'just better nick.'

Rudi turned the pick-up round and backed it up close to the doors. He ran out the winch cable and connected it to the helicopter and we began half dragging and half pushing it out of the building. It was covered in a thin layer of red dust and its body panels were a jigsaw of repaired and reclaimed pieces, suggesting it had had a hard and bullet-riddled life, but the rotor hubs were greased and, when I opened the engine covers, the turbines looked well maintained.

'It looks better than the other one,' I said. 'Where's the engineer?'

Grizz smiled. 'You're looking at him.'

'I thought you were the door gunner,' I said.

'That too. Versatility is the first rule of these kind of ops.'

'So why keep it here? What's wrong with the airport in Freetown?'

'If we left it there, it would be flogged by the first government minister who was short of a few quid. This way it's under our control.'

'Hardly,' I said. 'It's still guarded by government soldiers.'

He smiled. 'But the government doesn't pay them. We do. If the President says one thing and I say another, they'll do what I say.'

Rudi jumped down from the pick-up and disappeared into the gloom of the hangar. He returned rolling a drum of aviation fuel and began topping up the tanks as Tom, Grizz and I began a detailed check of the heli. Layla settled herself to wait in the shade, but a queue of soldiers formed next to her. All complained of aches and pains and pestered her for medicine. They wore a baffling variety of uniforms, collaged together with multicoloured T-shirts and sandals cut from old tyres. Their weapons were a similar mixture, but the guns did at least look well maintained.

It took us an hour to check the heli. The oil pressure on one of the engines was low and, as Grizz tinkered with it, I strolled over and sat next to Layla, who had just sent her last patient away.

'You had quite a queue there,' I said.

'It's the same wherever I go.'

'So what do you do?'

She met my gaze. 'Treat the sick ones as far as I'm able, and give the others a placebo—you'd be amazed how well it works.'

'What brought you to Sierra Leone?' I said.

'I'm a medic.'

'I know, but why here?'

'Why not? They need all the help they can get. Sierra Leone should be one of the richest countries in the world; it has platinum, gold, iron ore and diamonds. But it's the poorest country on earth. The national wealth's all held by foreign corporations or in Swiss bank accounts. By the time the mining companies'—she glanced at me—'and their mercenaries, the President, the army officers, government officials and rebels have had their share, there's precious little left. Know what they call the mining district? The Wild West. Officially, two million carats of diamonds are being exported every year, but even on the most conservative estimates, for every one legally exported, another two are smuggled across the border. There are no diamonds in Liberia and yet there are more diamond merchants in Monrovia than there are in Amsterdam.

'Of course, some of the theft is institutional. The government has no foreign currency reserves, so Decisive Measures are paid in mineral rights. They now get sixty per cent of the diamonds. Once they'd done that deal, they lost whatever interest they had in fighting the rebels. All they want to do is protect their diamond concessions.'

'And Medicaid International?'

'Are willing to get involved in places where no one else will. We can't change things but we can at least help to ease the misery of people who have nowhere else to turn.' She frowned. 'That's me. What persuaded you to join the mercenaries?'

'They don't like to be called that, but—'

'But that's what they are, hired killers.'

'So are all soldiers.'

'And pilots.'

'And pilots.' I paused, seeing in my mind the burning woman with her arms outstretched. I hurried on, trying to banish the image from my mind. 'Yes, sure. We're all trained to fight and kill; it's the last resort, but that's our job and sometimes we have to do it. In peacetime we're hated for it and in wartime people love us for it. But we're doing our government's bidding.'

'Mercenaries aren't.'

'Some aren't. Companies like Decisive Measures are. They're here to defend the diamond mines, but by doing that they're also keeping the rebels at bay. They're like the armed forces, but at one remove, doing the jobs the UK doesn't want to be seen doing for itself.'

She looked across at Rudi, who was cleaning and oiling his rifle. 'Like killing Africans.'

'That's not why I'm here. I'm here because I don't want to see . . .' My voice trailed away. 'Decisive Measures would say we're here to protect Western interests.' I changed tack. 'Listen, I'm a trained military pilot. I've left the RAF; what else can I do?'

'Why did you leave?'

I ducked the question. 'It's a job, it's money, but please don't call me a hired killer. I'm just flying people around, dropping guys on patrols, ferrying in supplies; it's like driving a bus or a truck.'

She pointed to the rocket pod under the body of the Huey. 'And where you come from buses are fitted with those, are they?'

'If you feel so strongly about this,' I said, 'why do you work with Decisive Measures yourself?'

'We have no helicopters and very few vehicles. So I treat Decisive Measures' mercenaries and the expats at the Bohara mine, because it also enables me to treat the African workers there and run clinics at some of the villages.' She stared at me. 'But that doesn't mean I condone what Decisive Measures do.'

Grizz wandered over, wiping the oil from his hands with a rag.

'Don't let Layla pile too much guilt on you, Jack. Mercenaries have been a part of Sierra Leone for centuries. Chiefs, merchants and traders all hired professional warriors; nothing's changed.' He paused. 'Now if you and Comrade Layla have finished your dialectical discussion, I've got a helicopter I'd like you to fly.'

Tom and I began the preflight checks. I scrambled into the cockpit. The dusty, scratched Perspex canopy was etched with the fine lines of stress patterns, casting a blurred halo around every object seen through it. I settled myself into the tiny, bone-hard seat and looked around. Tom and I had only a three-week familiarisation course on the Huey behind us, but already it felt as familiar to me as the driving seat of a family car.

I connected the helmet and radio and we ran through the first round of cockpit checks. Then I gave the wind-up signal to Tom and pressed the starter. The turbines coughed like a man clearing his lungs with the first cigarette of the day, and puffs of blue-black smoke drifted away behind us. Then they fired, roaring into life.

I shifted the lever into flight idle and the rotors began to turn, ponderously at first then accelerating to a blur. The noise increased to a thunder and a cloud of dust rose, obscuring the compound.

We made the last round of preflight checks, a rapid-fire exchange of question and response—fuel, hydraulic pressures, oil temperature, turbine outlet temperature, torque gauge and oil pressure.

Checks complete, I flicked the intercom switch. 'All ready?'

The answers came back at once. 'I'm ready,' Tom said.

'Ready in the back,' Grizz said.

I raised the collective and we lifted clear of the ground. The Huey was an old model, the workhorse of the US forces in Vietnam, but it was solid, well engineered and reliable.

I glanced across at Tom. 'Happy?'

'As happy as I can be seven hours' flying time from the King's Head.'

We made the short hop to Freetown airport and loaded the heli with supplies from Decisive Measures' storage bunkers. Then we took off again, tracking the road we had taken that morning. We passed the base and flew east over a plain of red earth and elephant grass studded with brown huts as round and fat as mushrooms.

Clumps of tall trees cast dark pools of shadow onto the baking earth and a broad river wound its way down from the distant mountains. Its banks were lined with trees, but beyond their shade the surface of the water sparkled like silver in the glare of the sun.

Layla leaned through from the cab, resting an arm on the back of my seat. 'What do you think?'

'Looks great, doesn't it?' I said.

'From here, maybe,' Tom said. 'Get down there with just the tsetse flies, mosquitoes and rebels for company and see how great it is.'

Layla stared at him. 'Perhaps you should reserve judgment until you've actually seen the place and met the people.'

'I don't need to. I already know what it's going to be like.'

'It must be nice to be so certain about everything.'

'Don't worry about him,' I said. 'He's got a mind like a steel trap—it's permanently closed.'

She stayed where she was, standing silent, watching me flying the Huey. 'It looks unbelievably complicated,' she said.

I glanced over my shoulder and smiled at her. 'It's not really. When we're airborne there are only four controls that matter—the rudders, the throttle, the collective and the cyclic.' I pointed towards the floor of the cockpit. 'The rudders are controlled by those foot pedals.

'On my left'—I waggled the control slightly—'is the collective. It increases and decreases the pitch angle of the rotors—pull it up and the heli rises, lower it and the heli goes down. The throttle grips are on the end of the collective—you twist power on and off.

'The cyclic is this long, thin stick that comes out of the cockpit floor between my legs. Whichever way you tilt the cyclic—forward, backward, left or right—the disc of the rotors, and therefore the heli itself, will tilt in the same direction.

'That's really all there is to it . . . except that none of the controls can be operated in isolation—not if you want to stay airborne. Movements of the cyclic and the collective have to be synchronised.'

We flew east for another hour, as the terrain grew steadily higher and rougher below us. Finally we climbed towards the last steep ridge separating us from the Bohara Valley. As we cleared the ridge line, I gasped at the desolation below us.

Whole forests had been felled, the ground cleared and levelled and then stripped to the bedrock. A river had been diverted and a huge dam built, flooding a vast area with water that was a sickly shade of orange. Manmade mountains of crushed rock, the tailings from the mine workings, rose hundreds of feet, bare of any vegetation. As far as my eyes could see, nothing grew in the entire lower valley.

A few antlike figures scurried around the monstrous machines gouging at the ground. Enormous draglines ripped at the diamond-bearing gravels, biting out tens of tons of rock at a time. Massive dumper trucks moved in an unending procession down to a smoke-belching mill, where they dumped gravel onto conveyor belts as wide as roads that disappeared into the gaping maw of the plant.

More conveyor belts moved the debris away, building fresh spoil heaps that seemed to grow as I watched them, and a torrent of discoloured water flowed constantly from an opening at the base of the mill. In the far distance beyond the mine I could see an ugly sprawling town, an island of a few concrete buildings rising from an ocean of mud huts and tarpaper shacks.

A much smaller shantytown surrounded the perimeter fences of the mining compound. The outer fence was a surreal combination of US cavalry fort and Belfast army base—a wooden palisade of sharpened stakes topped by a tangle of barbed wire. Inside the palisade was an altogether more modern fortification: a chain-link perimeter fence topped with coils of razor wire.

Right at the heart of the compound inside the fences was a helipad of beaten red earth.

CHAPTER 3

I circled the compound, determining the best approach to the landing site, clear of the worst obstacles and heading into the wind.

I came in and pushed the nose of the heli upwards, flaring towards the landing. The downwash threw up such a dense cloud of red dust that I had to use the artificial horizon indicator to hold the craft level. Turbulence from the ground threw the helicopter around as we descended the last few feet. I levelled the nose but still made a heavy landing, thumping down onto the springs.

I shut down the engines, stripped off my flying helmet and wiped the sweat from my forehead as the wind from the slowing rotors blew away the last traces of the dust cloud. Then I climbed stiffly down from the cockpit to join the others.

A tall, dark-haired man was waiting to greet us. He was in civilian clothes, but he wore them like a uniform; everything from his immaculately parted and combed hair to his unrolled sleeves and sharp-creased trousers marked him out as an ex-army officer.

'Welcome to Bohara,' he said. 'I'm Colonel Henry Pleydell, CEO of Decisive Measures, but don't worry'—he did his best to put a twinkle in his eye—'this is just a flying visit. We're here to protect the integrity of this site and ensure the smooth running of one of the world's largest diamond mines.' He gestured to the town just visible in the distance. 'That was a cluster of half a dozen huts when diamonds were discovered here. It's now a town of seventy-five thousand people, the biggest in the country after Freetown.

'Most of the processes are automated. There are few hand operations because of the opportunities for pilfering they would allow. There are thousands of illegal miners.' His lips pursed in distaste. 'They work at night in the hope of avoiding our security and they make a bloody nuisance of themselves. Areas levelled for mechanical mining one day are often scarred with hand-dug pits by the next morning.' He studied them for a moment. 'Well, I hope you enjoy your stay here.'

As he turned to consult one of the mining engineers, I took a look at his kingdom. All round the inside of the outer palisade were palm-roofed sheds that looked like Second World War Japanese prison huts.

Layla followed my gaze. 'The native workers live in them,' she said. 'The mine operates twenty-four hours a day, seven days a week and the miners work twelve hours on, twelve hours off. The day shift sleep in the beds the night shift have just vacated. Some of their wives and dependants live in the shanties just outside the wire . . .'

She broke off as Pleydell began shaking hands all round, then he climbed into a heavily armoured Land-Rover. Six mercenaries took up gun positions on it before it was driven out of the gates.

'So it's back to the golf course for the colonel then,' Grizz said.

I continued my scrutiny of the compound. Eight shipping containers had been stacked together in a double-tiered block in the centre. Door and window openings had been cut into them and steel grilles had been welded over the windows. The whole construction was surrounded by an earth mound, capped with a sandbag wall. It was obviously the last redoubt.

A row of single-storey breeze-block houses surrounded it, the accommodation for the expatriate workers. Awnings round the sides gave the houses a little shade. There were sun loungers, swing seats and barbecues on the stoops, and inside each house, no doubt, were televisions, freezers, and fridges full of cold beer.

Layla peeled off to begin her clinic, a row of Africans waiting patiently next to the fire pit where the cooking was done. The rest of us walked over to the stacked containers and filed through a gap in the sandbag walls. Grizz showed us around. The mining company used the upper tier for offices. The front half of the lower tier served as a combined mess hall, satellite TV lounge, briefing room and relaxation area for the mercenaries, and an end section was used as a dormitory. Rudi had already bagged a spare bunk and made himself comfortable. Tom and I chose a couple as far from him as possible.

Most of the other soldiers were watching videos, an arsenal of weapons propped against the walls. We were introduced to them: white officers and NCOs, commanding black troops. Few of the latter were in evidence and I wondered if their quarters were with the black workers beyond the wire. From their accents, the majority of the white soldiers were Rudi's fellow countrymen, but there were five Englishmen, two of whom claimed to be ex-SAS.

'I'm from Hereford—enough said,' one growled as he crushed my hand in an iron handshake. 'Call me Raz, everybody else does.' He was at least a couple of years younger than me, with keen blue eyes and a square, pugnacious chin.

'That's my mate Reuben,' he said, pointing out another young mercenary with a round, moon face and a facial tic that made him blink his eyes in a constant rapid motion. It gave him an air of permanent surprise. He raised an arm in greeting, blinked, smiled, blinked again and turned his attention back to the television.

'The thick-looking one is Hendrik,' Raz said, gesturing towards a bull of a man picking his teeth with the point of a knife, who gave us a curt nod at the mention of his name. 'Don't let his table manners put you off. He's not a bad guy—for a South African.'

The three of them were the only ones who bothered to shift their eyes away from the television screen. So we left them to their videos and moved back to the dining area. Grizz reached into a battered old fridge and passed Tom and me a beer.

I dropped my voice. 'Are those two real Hereford or bullshitters?'

'Bullshitters. One of the guys is an ex-Para. The rest are infantrymen or South African veterans of the bush wars against the ANC.'

There was a sudden burst of firing outside. It provoked a flurry of activity. Soldiers grabbed their helmets and weapons and sprinted for the door. Grizz strode across the room and ran outside.

There was no further shooting and Grizz and the others soon returned. 'No big deal,' he said. 'A couple of rebels taking a few pot shots. A patrol's gone out, but they'll have legged it by now.'

Remembering that Layla had been outside right through the shooting, I hurried out into the bright sunlight. The queue waiting for treatment had dwindled to a handful of people. I stepped back into the shade by the door and watched Layla as she worked.

Some of the African workers had brought their wives and children into the compound to be treated, and even the smallest child, a little boy, showed no fear as Layla examined him. With one hand she stroked his forehead as she tested his distended stomach wall with the other. She gave the parents a reassuring smile, but I saw her bleak look as they turned away with the medicine she had given them.

She started as I stepped out of the shadows next to her. 'Sorry,' I said. 'Didn't mean to startle you. Was that a placebo?'

She nodded. 'But it won't do any good in that case.'

'Is there anything you can do for him?'

'Not really . . .'

'We could fly him to Freetown.'

She looked up in surprise. 'You obviously haven't read the Decisive Measures manual—no inessential passengers allowed.'

'Sod the manual. If it's a matter of life and death, let's do it and worry about it afterwards.'

'Thanks.' I felt the cool touch of her fingers on my arm. 'But it's not that simple. Even in Freetown there are neither the drugs nor the expertise to cure him, and he'll be far from his parents and his village if—when—the worst happens. It's better that he stays here.'

By the time she had seen her last patient, night was falling.

'I've never got used to how quickly the sun sets in the tropics,' I said. 'I really miss those long summer evenings back home.'

'Me too.' She fell silent, staring up at the darkening sky.

'Where is home for you?'

'Don't laugh, I'm an Essex girl; not the best place to grow up for someone of my—' She hesitated. 'Of my background.'

'What do you mean?'

'What do you think I mean?' She shot me a suspicious look. 'My mother was a nurse. She met my dad when he was in hospital after an accident. He'd been an engineer in Guyana; the only job he could get in England was on the assembly line at Dagenham. Maybe things are different there now, but it seemed to me that I was always too black for some and too white for others.' She fell silent and gave a slow shake of her head. 'I don't know why I'm even telling you this. You're no different—just another white mercenary that fancies his chances with me.'

'That's not true.'

'Isn't it?'

I looked around. It was now full dark. A solitary soldier was patrolling the perimeter wire, his boots scuffing in the dust. There seemed to be no one else around. The normal noise of the African bush—the chatter of monkeys, the croaking of frogs and the whine and buzz of a billion insects—was absent. In this valley of desolation, almost nothing moved except men and machines.

The night had a strange beauty of its own, however. The stars dusting the sky overhead were mirrored by a myriad pinpricks of light, moving slowly through the mine workings like glow-worms in the darkness of some vast cave.

'What are they?' I said.

'The illicit miners. They work at night by candle- or lantern-light. They dig out the gravel and carry it in baskets on their heads to the nearest stream. They sieve and jig it, then turn it upside-down and handpick any diamonds.' She paused. 'If they have time before the guard patrols chase them away or shoot them.'

'There must be at least a thousand of them.'

'Why be surprised? There's no other work to be had. The mines have destroyed or flooded most of the farmland, and wrecked the fisheries too.' She searched my face for a moment. 'If you want to see the real Sierra Leone, come with me tomorrow. I'm doing a clinic in Boroyende, a village a few miles north. Some of what you'll see is far from pleasant but it can be inspiring. It'll give you an insight into what the country could be like if the war ever ends and the mines start to be run for the benefit of Sierra Leone, not Britain and America.'

'All right,' I said. 'I'd like that.'

She gave me a dazzling smile. 'Good. Now I'm pretty tired and we have an early start in the morning. I'm going to get some sleep.'

She walked across the compound to one of the breeze-block houses. As she closed the door and walked through the house I saw her shadow outlined against the blinds. I stood watching for some time before I went back into the container building.

Grizz gave me an old-fashioned look when I asked him if I could go with Layla. 'I've told you, you're wasting your time with her.'

I remained impassive. 'So may I go?'

'Yeah, I suppose so. I could do with the time up here to lick these useless bastards into shape. But don't get captured by the rebels. They're not that far from Boroyende. Take a rifle as well as your pistol, and ammunition. And be back in time to get us back to Freetown before dark.'

As I walked to my bunk, Grizz's mocking voice came floating after me. 'Oh and Jack? Want Tom to come with you for company?'

'If he wants to,' I said.

'No chance,' Tom said. 'I'll let you do the tourist bit. I'm quite happy here, thank you very much.'

I smiled to myself as I stretched out on my bunk.

I closed my eyes and lay there replaying in my mind the shape of Layla's body outlined against the blind, trying to hold off sleep as long as I could, knowing that the familiar nightmare would once more be lying in wait.

I GOT UP as soon as the first grey light of dawn showed in the sky, but by the time I'd showered and grabbed some breakfast, Layla was already waiting for me.

'We drive part of the way and then walk the rest,' she said. She climbed into the driving seat of one of the mine's pick-ups.

'The mining companies do have some uses, then,' I said.

She gave me a sharp look. 'It's part of the deal with Medicaid.'

We drove out of the gates of the inner and outer compounds through the shantytown outside and up a steep track skirting the spoil heaps from the mine and climbing towards the ridge. The narrow summit plateau bridged two vastly different worlds. Behind was bare rock, polluted water, the din of heavy machinery and ugly shantytowns shrouded in a pall of dust and smoke. Ahead was a lush valley, a patchwork of villages and small fields, surrounded by broad swaths of dense forest. Only as we began to descend the hillside did I see the scars of war on the land—smashed buildings and abandoned fields slowly reverting to forest.

We drove on towards the distant mountains. The vegetation grew sparser and more patchy and the few tribespeople looked desperately poor and thin. Some men were dressed in rags, others wore no clothes at all. All carried pangas—bush knives.

'They subsist on slash-and-burn agriculture,' Layla said. 'In the last few years, the fighting has forced many of them to flee before they've even been able to harvest their crops.' She shrugged. 'Some say it's deliberate; the rebels and the government forces drive them out, then share the crops between themselves.'

Some villages had disappeared altogether, their sites only detectable from the overgrown orange and mango trees and the circles of burnt, blackened earth where huts had been torched.

Layla pulled up at one set of ruins and parked the pick-up.

I picked up my rifle and a rucksack heavy with ammunition, and followed Layla through the ghost village and out along a path leading into the forest. It was green and cool at first, after the heat of the sun, but before long our clothing was soaked with sweat.

We walked for an hour. Eventually the path widened and small, cultivated fields began to appear, niches carved out of the enclosing wall of the forest. We passed women with head-loads of firewood, and men carrying hoes and pangas. All gazed warily at my rifle, but broke into broad welcoming smiles as they recognised Layla. Many of them embraced her and the women held up babies for her inspection, their faces glowing with pride. Layla was soon surrounded and she stopped to carry out her first impromptu treatment at the side of the track.

I walked the last few yards to the village alone. It appeared to be deserted. The path ended in a clearing of beaten earth. A breadfruit tree stood in the centre, casting a pool of shade. Around the edge of the clearing were a dozen mud huts, roofed with palm thatch.

I glanced inside the first hut; it was empty. The earth floor was swept clean, the cooking pots and bowls were stacked on a shelf nailed between two of the stout bush poles supporting the roof, and the sleeping mats were neatly rolled.

The next hut must have belonged to the village carpenter. There were tools with the dull glint of age and the patina of constant use, and a handful of nails burnished where they had been hammered to straighten them. There were also scraps of wire, rope and string and a broken saw blade refitted with an improvised handle. The furniture included a beautifully carved and jointed rocking chair that any English craftsman would have been proud to have made.

I stepped back outside and a moment later Layla joined me. 'That was quite a welcome you got back there,' I said.

'I was based in Boroyende for three years when I first came out here and I've been doing clinics in the village ever since—eight years all told. I've nursed them through a few illnesses, delivered their children, come to their weddings.' A shadow passed over her face. 'And the funerals of those I could do nothing for. They're good people.'

She walked to the centre of the clearing and called out. Slowly the frightened people began to reappear from the forest. A grizzled, white-haired old man led the way. He embraced Layla and talked animatedly to her in the local language.

She replied, then gestured to me. What she said must have been reassuring, for the old man gave a broad smile and shook my hand.

'This is Njama,' she said to me. 'He understands a little English.'

I introduced myself and made the ritual congratulations on the village and the crops. He smiled, bowing his head in acknowledgment, then clapped his hands and signalled for food to be brought.

They had little enough but it was shared without a second thought.

As people moved around the village, I noticed that several of them had only one arm. 'What happened to them?' I said.

'The rebels,' Layla said. 'Anyone suspected of supporting the wrong side at the election had an arm severed in punishment. You get the idea: cut off the arm that voted for the government. Thousands of people were mutilated. You see them everywhere. Worse things are done every day here.' She looked past me and called out to a boy who was loitering at the edge of the clearing. He hesitated, then made his way over to us. He seemed no more than nine years old, but, when his gaze met mine, the sad, world-weary eyes of a far older man looked back at me.

'Kaba is from a different tribe,' Layla said. 'But Njama's people have taken him in. He has no family of his own.' She stroked his hair as she spoke. 'His tribe are traditional hunters. At first, they fought to defend their villages against the army and the rebels alike, but then they were recruited by the government as mercenaries or forcibly conscripted by the rebels.

'When the rebels attack a village, they usually kill the adults and take the children. The boys are formed into "Small Boys Units", brutalised, drugged and sent into battle. They're highly valued as soldiers because they're fearless. They go into battle believing that bullets cannot hurt them.'

'And has their belief in their own invulnerability survived the evidence of their friends dying around them?'

'They are told that if one of them dies it is because he has broken one of the myriad rules governing their way of fighting. They are not allowed to have sex with a woman before they fight. Kaba was too young anyway. He speaks good English. Let him tell you his story.' She gave the boy a gentle smile and held his hand as he began to speak.

'I was a captain in one of the Small Boys Units,' he said. 'Our job was to cut off people's hands, to kill and burn houses. I was promoted because I did it well. The rebels gave us tablets with our food. They gave us power; they made us brave.'

'They feed them a mixture of amphetamines, marijuana, alcohol and gunpowder,' Layla said.

'It made our hearts strong,' Kaba said. 'We were not afraid of anything. Sometimes we drank the blood of those we had killed. The men ate the hearts and livers, as well. We were told it gave us power.'

I shuddered. 'What happened to your parents?'

'They are dead.' He hesitated, twisting his hands together. 'I killed them. The rebels told me, "Kill your mother and father, and your brothers and sisters, or we will kill you."'

He pulled his hand from Layla's and walked back across the clearing.

The food had arrived, so we sat down to eat. Kaba's story had left me with little appetite, but out of politeness I took a little of the dried, smoked fish and rice.

'As you can see, it's a limited but adequate and healthy diet,' Layla said, 'provided they can harvest their rice. They also eat fruit, potato leaf, cassava and okra, and catch fish in traps.'

A jug of palm oil was passed round and poured over the food. 'It makes it more palatable,' Layla said. 'They use palm oil for everything. They cook with it and preserve food in it; fish in oil keeps for months. It's also mixed with ashes and used as soap.'

Njama began to speak to me, pausing to allow Layla to translate. 'We have lived here for many generations, our land is good, but we have lost too many people. We dare not stray far from the village. We have to clear and cultivate where we can, when we can.'

As soon as we had finished eating, a queue of patients formed for Layla to examine. As she worked, Njama took my arm and led me away across the village towards his hut. He ushered me inside.

His sons, four beetle-browed men ranging in age from twenty to thirty, I guessed, followed us in. It was a few minutes before I realised that three of the four had had their right hands severed at the wrist.

The sons stared at me but did not speak as their father proudly showed me around. The internal walls were just bare mud. The men's weapons—pangas, spears and an old hunting rifle—hung from pegs and nails driven into the walls. A line of shell casings held water, rice, dried fish and palm oil, and metal from the doors and body panels of wrecked vehicles had been beaten into plates and bowls.

Njama raised his eyes to the ceiling, his face glowing with pride. I followed his gaze and found myself staring at a fly-specked electric light bulb dangling from the thatched roof.

Njama pulled a switch. The light bulb lit with a feeble glow, casting a fitful light into the recesses of the hut.

I shook my head in disbelief. 'How?'

He laughed, then led me out and around the side of the hut. We walked down to the river, where the rusting wheel of a truck had been set up on an axle attached to the river bank. Rough metal paddle blades, cut from the truck's bodywork, had been fixed at intervals around the rim. They spun in the current, powering a dynamo.

I smiled. 'You remind me of my father. When I was a small boy, he was always out in his shed in our garden, trying to find uses for bits of metal and wire or the motor from an old vacuum cleaner.'

I reached in my pocket and took out my Swiss Army penknife. I showed him the different tools and blades, then folded it up and pressed it into his hand. His sons clustered around him, exclaiming at each new blade or tool that he produced from the handle, like a conjuror pulling rabbits from a hat.

When I made as if to leave, Njama detained me for a moment. He stared hard into my eyes. 'You will not take Layla away from us?'

I shrugged, embarrassed. 'I hardly know her. We work together, that's all.'

He smiled. 'But I have seen the way you look at her . . . I think you will bring her happiness.' He spread his hands, encompassing the whole village. 'And if you do, you will have many friends here.'

I was silent most of the way back from the village, mulling over what I had seen and heard. Layla glanced at me frequently as we walked along the forest path and drove back to Bohara.

'It's both better and worse than I imagined,' I said at last. 'They have nothing and yet they have everything they need. But when you hear Njama or Kaba talk . . .' I paused, seeing Kaba's young-old face in my mind as he recounted those unspeakable horrors in his expressionless voice. 'I wish there was something I could do for them.'

'There is. But you have to be willing to work for someone like Medicaid for the benefit of the villagers, not the mercenaries and the mining corporations. I'm not sure you'd be able to do that.'

It was more of a question than a statement. I didn't reply.

CHAPTER 4

We collected Grizz and Tom from Bohara and flew back to Camp 17 that afternoon. The flight was uneventful, and as I swung in towards the base I was thinking about a cold beer when there was a sudden silence. The whine of the turbines had disappeared. In its place there was just the rush of wind and the slowing noise of the rotors. Then there was the scream of a siren.

I shouted a warning. 'Engine failure! Prepare for autorotative landing. Get back in the cab, Layla. Hold on for your life!'

A helicopter in free fall drops at around 1,700 feet per minute. Already under 200 feet, I had less than six seconds to react to the power failure, identify a clear area and land in it. Instinctively I rammed the collective full down to neutralise the pitch angle of the rotors. If they remained at flying angle the blades would slow and stop immediately. Rigid, they would then fold up like a bird folding its wings, with similar results. But once I'd made sure they were flat, the uprushing air would continue to turn the rotors and provide enough uplift to cushion the impact. That was the theory, at least.

There was a clear, roughly level patch of land just inside the perimeter of the base. I aimed straight at it, and fifty feet from the ground I hauled back on the cyclic to flare the heli and bleed off the forward air speed down to zero. I kept the nose in the flare as we plummeted groundwards, then at the last minute I levelled it.

We crashed down with a sickening thud. My teeth crunched together and my neck was whipped back into the headrest. The heli bottomed on its springs and gave an almost human groan as it bounced up again. We came to a rest, canted at a slight angle.

The rotors wound down and stopped and there was a sudden silence. I was already tearing at my straps and twisting to look back into the cab. The cockpit was cushioned by powerful shock absorbers, but the cab had almost no protection. People in the back often suffered crushed vertebrae after an autorotative landing.

'Layla.' I struggled through the narrow gap between the seats and into the cab. She was still strapped in, her eyes closed, her face deathly pale. 'Layla!'

Her eyes flickered open. 'I'm all right. I was just scared to death, that's all.' She started to unbuckle her harness.

'Don't move until you're sure your back's all right.'

She made some cautious exploratory movements of her neck and shoulders, then eased herself away from her seat. 'I'm OK.'

'Thank God for that.' I began to help her towards the door.

'Well, don't worry about me, will you?' Grizz said.

'Sorry, Grizz. Are you all right?'

'As a matter of fact I am, yes, but thanks for asking anyway.'

Tom began to giggle and within seconds we were all creased up with laughter. The release of tension made it seem the greatest joke we'd ever heard.

We clambered down from the heli and began looking it over.

'Nothing broken as far as I can see,' I said, 'but I'd rather not take it up again until we know why the engines cut out like that.'

'I'm with you on that,' Grizz said. 'I'll get the guys here to haul it back to the hangar, then I'll strip it down and put it back together.'

'What about us?'

'I'll need one of you to give me a hand. The other one can take Layla back to Freetown and come back out here tomorrow.'

I turned to look at Tom.

He stared at me for a moment. 'All right, you win. I'll stay here.'

I tried hard not to look too pleased.

Grizz handed me a rifle and some spare clips. 'It never hurts to be prepared. And take this radio so we can stay in touch.'

'All right. But I don't want you bothering me all the time when I'm trying to relax.'

He gave an enigmatic smile.

'What?'

'Nothing. Just have a nice night, that's all.'

Layla studied him, arms folded, head on one side. Then she looked around the dusty, fly-blown base and laughed. 'I tell you what, Grizz. We'll be hard-pressed to have a worse night than you.'

WE REACHED FREETOWN in the late afternoon. The sky was pale, almost white, and the low sun was a faint ghost of itself, obscured by dust. The months of rain had at last given way to the dry harmattan wind, laden with fine sand carried from the Sahara. As we drove down the hill to the city centre, it hung like fog in the air.

Before I got out of the pick-up, I wrapped a piece of rag round my face like a mask, but almost at once I could feel the dust in my nose and taste it in my mouth. The air was full of creaking sounds as the wooden buildings dried in the wind.

When I reached my hotel room, I found that the dust had seeped in round the edge of the windows and suffused my books and clothes. It had even passed through the mosquito net and settled like talc on my bedding.

After a quick shower I met Layla for dinner. The hotel menu had a choice of smoked fish, rice and okra—or an unidentified stew.

We chose fish and, more in hope than expectation, I ordered a bottle of wine. I took a dubious sip, then another. 'It's delicious,' I said, 'full-bodied and Lebanese—just like the hotel owner.'

She smiled, and the stress lines etched into her face disappeared.

'That's better,' I said. 'Leave your problems outside and relax.'

'I get the feeling that's not something you're very good at doing.'

I bowed my head. 'Guilty,' I said.

She studied me. 'So why are you here? I'll grant you this, you don't seem like the other mercenaries. They're pushing forty. Yet what are you? Twenty-eight? Twenty-nine?'

I nodded. 'Right first time.'

'You could have had another ten years in the RAF, couldn't you? So why leave? And why come here?'

'I guess I needed a change.' It sounded lame even to me.

She waited in silence for me to continue.

'I—I just wanted a steady job, I suppose. No excitement—'

'And no responsibilities?'

'That too.'

She gave a wry smile. 'Sierra Leone isn't exactly noted for its quietness, and when things go wrong here, even those on the sidelines find themselves involved whether they like it or not.'

I poured us each another glass of wine. 'So what about you?' I said. 'Why are you here?'

'I got into trouble at my last posting. I expressed my opinions a bit too forcefully to a politician. It took some hasty diplomacy to prevent the entire medical team being expelled. I was lucky not to be sacked, but this was the worst posting they could think of.' She smiled. 'Funnily enough, despite all the deprivation and violence, I love it here. I feel as if I belong.'

The hotel owner cleared away our plates and brought tiny cups of thick, black Lebanese coffee with powdered milk and gritty sugar. We sat talking late into the evening, long after the other diners had left. As we said good night outside my room, I leaned forward to kiss her.

She let my lips brush against hers, but when I tried to prolong the embrace, she pushed me away. 'Let's just keep it friendly, Jack,' she said. 'I'd need to know an awful lot more about you before I'd even consider being the next notch on your bedpost.'

'I know that,' I said. 'I didn't—' But she was already walking down the corridor.

When I got into bed, I lay staring into the darkness for a long time but, like almost every night since Kosovo, the familiar nightmare was waiting for me when I at last fell asleep. This time there was a difference, however: a hand began beckoning from the flames and a man's voice shouted over and over, 'Come in. Come in.'

I awoke. The voice continued. 'Jack, come in. Jack, come in.'

I lay there trying to make sense of it, as cold sweat trickled down my forehead. Then I sat upright, clambered out of bed and began to rummage through the pitch-dark room for the radio Grizz had given me. I found it at last, buried under my discarded clothes.

'This is Jack. What's happening, Grizz?'

'There's shit flying at Bohara. A big rebel assault. The guys have taken casualties. Get Layla, and get out here to the base. We must take the heli and go as soon as we can.'

'But the heli's not fit to fly until it's been fixed.'

'We've sorted it,' he said. 'Now get out here pronto.'

I dragged my clothes on then ran and pounded on Layla's door.

A sleepy voice answered and she came to the door wrapped in a towel. Even half asleep she looked heart-stoppingly beautiful.

'Grizz has been on the radio,' I said. 'There's trouble at Bohara. We've got to get going at once.'

She stared at me for a moment. 'What sort of trouble?'

'The rebels.'

She turned back into the room. Through the half-open door, I saw the sheen of starlight on her skin as she dropped the towel and pulled on a T-shirt and jeans. A moment later she was hurrying out of the door, holding her medical bags.

We ran downstairs and out into the darkness.

I revved the engine of the pick-up and we drove off through the deserted streets. Layla sat silent in the passenger seat staring out through the windscreen, her lip caught between her teeth.

'Are you all right?' I said.

'What? Yes, sorry, I was just thinking about Njama's people, wondering if they're safe.'

We left the city and began the climb through open country towards the mountains. As we approached the bend where we'd encountered the roadblock, I slipped the radio and my pistol under the seat. The rifle that Grizz had given me was still sitting in the hotel room. I cursed, but it was too late to go back for it now.

I was only half expecting the barrier to be manned, but as we rounded the corner, I brought the pick-up to a juddering halt. A dozen heavily armed men stood guard on the barrier. They levelled their rifles at us as soon as we came into view.

'This doesn't look too clever,' I said.

'Give them some cigarettes and we should be all right,' Layla said.

I wound down the window and held out the carton as we stopped in front of the barrier. The soldiers looked tired and edgy. One of them—the leader, I guessed, going by the mirrored sunglasses he wore like a badge of office—walked to the door of the pick-up, took the cigarettes from me, then jerked his head. 'Get out of the car.'

We got out and the soldier searched us in turn. I saw Layla flinch as he handled her breasts while pretending to search for concealed weapons. Then he stepped back and signalled to two of the others to search the vehicle.

They handed him Layla's medical bag, then one of them found the radio and pistol under the seat.

The leader turned the pistol over in his hands. 'What is this?' he said angrily. 'Who are you? What are you doing here?'

'As you can see from our medical bag, we're doctors with

Medicaid International,' I said before Layla could speak. 'We're on our way to treat a very ill patient. Please let us pass.'

'Since when do doctors carry guns?'

I spread my hands. 'These are dangerous times. I carry it only for protection from robbers and bandits.'

He studied me for a moment. 'Where is this patient of yours?'

'At the army camp at the top of the hill.'

He stiffened. 'He is a soldier, then.'

'No,' I said. 'She is a civilian. The soldiers took her to the camp because she was so ill.'

'What is wrong with her?'

Layla jumped in before I could reply. 'She is with child. She has been in labour for almost two days. If we do not get to her soon, both she and her baby will die.' She held his gaze. 'Please. Imagine if this was your wife and your baby. One day it might be.'

He hesitated, then gave a curt nod. With some show of reluctance, his men began moving the barricade.

'My pistol and my radio?' I said.

He shook his head. 'Radios are the tools of spies, not doctors.'

I thought about arguing, then let it go. 'And my pistol?'

He slipped it into his pocket. 'You will have no need of this. I and my men control this road. We permit no thieves or bandits.' His smile challenged me to argue with him if I dared.

We got back into the pick-up. I drove away up the hill.

As we passed out of sight of them I heard machine-gun fire coming not from behind us but from somewhere in the darkness ahead.

I braked to a halt, switched off the lights, then put the pick-up in gear and began creeping forward again, steering only by the faint glow of the moonlight reflected from the surface of the road.

When we crested the brow of the hill, I saw a reddish glow away to our left. It pulsed and flickered, sending sparks spiralling upwards.

'The base,' Layla said. 'What do we do?'

I pulled the pick-up off the road into a small clearing at the edge of the forest. 'We go forward on foot and see what's going on.'

We climbed out and inched our way forward through the trees, stumbling over dead branches. I was soaked with sweat, as much from tension as the exertion in the heat of the night. Pumped up on adrenaline, I was hyperalert, straining my eyes to see into the darkness ahead, imagining rebel soldiers hiding behind every bush.

We crawled the last few yards through the undergrowth at the edge of the base. I raised my head a little and parted the branches in front of me, then flattened myself at once.

Not more than thirty yards away was a rebel position. Their commander was directing fire, shouting orders into the radios he held in either hand. Other groups of rebels were scattered around the perimeter and the heavy machine gun we had heard from the hill was set up a hundred yards to his right.

Inside the base, the huts nearest to us were ablaze, but through the smoke I could glimpse the hangar where the heli was. It looked intact and was still protected by a cordon of defenders.

Even so, the position seemed hopeless. There were no more than a couple of dozen soldiers at Grizz's disposal and at least ten times that number of rebels.

'We have to get into the base,' I said. 'If I can get the Huey airborne we've a chance of driving these bastards off.'

'We can't,' Layla said. 'They've got it completely surrounded.'

'We've got to do something. If we just sit here, Grizz, Tom and everybody else will be slaughtered. We've got to create a diversion somehow. Come on.'

'Where are we going?'

'Back to the pick-up.'

CHAPTER 5

With the crash of gunfire reverberating in our ears, we retraced our steps through the forest.

Before I drove away, I ripped my shirtsleeve off, then unscrewed the cap from the fuel tank and dowsed the cloth in petrol. I left half of it protruding from the neck of the tank, then drove slowly, without lights, down the track to the base.

The thunder of gunfire grew louder and, as we rounded a bend, I saw the glare of burning buildings and the muzzle flashes of scores of weapons. I stopped the pick-up in the darkness beneath a clump of trees overhanging the track.

The rebel commander's position was directly ahead of me down the track, just beyond a parked truck. I turned my head and let my gaze travel slowly along the perimeter of the base, picking out the other groups of rebels.

I touched Layla's arm and pointed to a section of the fence almost midway between two groups of rebels. A tree grew close to the wire and the ground dipped down towards the fence, giving a little cover. 'That's the best place,' I said. I stripped off my flying jacket. 'Take that and sprint down to the fence. Wait under cover of the tree until the balloon goes up, then throw the jacket onto the barbed wire and climb over it.'

'And where will you be?'

'Right on your heels all the way.'

'It's too dangerous, Jack. Even if the rebels don't shoot us, when Grizz's men see us climbing over the wire, they're not going to wait for us to identify ourselves, they're just going to shoot us.'

'That's the chance we have to take. If we don't get into the base and get that heli airborne, they'll all be killed.'

I leaned across the seat and kissed her. She stared at me, then took my flying jacket and slipped out of the pick-up.

I watched her run down the slope to the tree, then I reversed along the track a hundred yards. I got out of the pick-up, found a good-sized rock and slipped it into the vehicle's footwell, then walked back to the tailgate. I struck a light, ignited the cloth trailing from the neck of the petrol tank and sprinted for the cab. I accelerated through first and second gears, then lined up the pick-up on its target, rolled the rock onto the accelerator, jamming it to the boards, and dived out of the side. The impact as I hit the ground drove the air from my lungs.

Still accelerating, the pick-up bucketed along the track and hit the rear corner of the truck. There was a beat of silence then a blast as the petrol tank exploded and fire erupted into the air. Before the glare had faded, I was running bent double down the slope.

I saw Layla throw the jacket onto the barbed wire and begin to climb. I reached the bottom as she struggled over, and heard her stifle a cry of pain as a barb spiked her hand. Then she was dropping to the ground on the other side.

I was almost at the top when I heard a shout from inside the base and a burst of gunfire was directed at me. A moment later I was also spotted by the rebels. Caught in the lethal crossfire from both sides, I threw myself forward. I felt the barbs ripping and tearing at me, then I was falling to the ground.

I landed heavily on my side, but staggered to my feet and was off, stumbling after Layla, running for cover as bullets cracked and whined around me. We flung ourselves into a hollow and lay still as bullets chewed at the earth above our heads.

I waited for a lull in the firing then, still in cover, I shouted, 'Grizz!' I raised my arms. There was an isolated shot, then silence. I straightened a little, and advanced a couple of feet out of cover. Four black soldiers had their guns levelled at my guts. I could see their puzzlement at my white skin.

Beyond them I saw Grizz with his back to me, crouching behind an earth mound and directing fire towards the far side of the compound. I heard Layla start to follow me. 'Not yet,' I said. 'Wait there.'

She ignored me and came alongside me, her arms also raised. I shouted again at the top of my voice. '*Grizz!*'

I saw him turn, stare at us, then shout at the soldiers. They kept us covered as we moved slowly forward. A moment later Grizz came sprinting towards us. He pushed past the soldiers, dragged us down behind the earth mound and grabbed us both in a bear hug. 'Thank God,' he said. 'I'd written you off. Can you get airborne and give us some help here?'

'Just watch me. Get your boys to give us some cover while we get the heli out. It will fly, won't it?'

'Let's hope so. We fixed it, but we've had no time to test it.'

'Guns?'

'Fully loaded. No time for the rocket pod, though.'

'Right.' I turned and ran at a crouch towards the hangar. Grizz followed. 'Where's Tom?' I called over my shoulder.

'You'll have to manage without him. He's been hit in the leg.'

We dragged the hangar doors open. I put on the night-vision

goggles and then fired up the engines while the heli was still inside the building. The defenders laid down a barrage of fire until Grizz gave them the signal, then a dozen of them dropped their weapons and ran to push the Huey out of the hangar into the open.

When the nose of the heli appeared the rebels redoubled their fire, raining down everything they had to try to stop the Huey getting airborne. Even though an embankment partly shielded it from the rebel fire, rounds were cracking and rattling on the heli's metal skin. I tried to force myself to concentrate on the controls in my hands.

As soon as the tips of the rotor arms cleared the hangar door, I gunned the engines. The rotors turned, blurred and accelerated into an unbroken disc overhead.

Grizz threw himself into the cab as the Huey lifted on its springs and then we were airborne. I banked hard away from the main concentration of rebels, climbing rapidly to 200 feet, then I swung round and came in low and fast at my first target, the rebel command position.

I heard the chatter of the mini-gun as Grizz opened up from the door of the cab, laying down a barrage of fire, but I held off with the nose gun until the cross hairs intersected on the left-hand man in the rebel group. Then I squeezed the trigger, easing the right rudder down to walk the line of fire right across the cluster of rebel troops. The nose guns thundered and I heard the heavy rattle of ejected cartridges and smelt smoke and the tang of cordite.

I was already banking to bring the next group of rebels into my sights: the men manning the heavy machine gun. I squeezed the trigger again, swinging the heli around to move the line of fire through the target. The ground below me shook and erupted. Clods of earth were flung high into the air and dust mingled with smoke.

A few rebels returned fire, but it was ragged stuff. They began running in all directions. I saw the commander jump into the truck and begin urging the driver back, but its way was blocked by the burnt-out pick-up. I lined up the guns and riddled the truck from bumper to bumper. It disappeared in a cloud of smoke and flame.

I pursued a group of fleeing rebels until I had emptied the guns, then banked around, back to the base.

We landed and I climbed down from the cockpit. Slowly the defenders began to emerge from behind the barricades.

Grizz slapped me on the back, 'Great shooting, ace.' His men fanned out across the base, pausing to examine each fallen rebel. There was a drumroll of single shots as the injured were finished off with a bullet in the head. I turned away.

Grizz caught my eye. 'That's the nature of war for all sides here,' he said. 'The Geneva Convention didn't make it this far. There's not enough medicine, food or anything else to supply your own side, let alone prisoners of war. So . . .' He put his forefinger against his temple and mimed pulling a trigger.

Layla emerged from a bunker looking drawn and deathly pale. We looked at each other. Grizz's face was a mass of cuts and bruises. I didn't paint too pretty a picture either.

'Where's Tom?' I said, suppressing a guilty twinge that I had only just thought about him.

Grizz gestured towards a low building alongside the hangar. 'He's in the hut there. Like I said, he's wounded, but he's OK, I think. He caught a bullet in the thigh, a flesh wound, but he made a lot of fuss about it—you know what pilots are like—so we dosed him up with morphine.' He switched his gaze to Layla. 'Now the heat's off, you can look him and the rest of the casualties over.'

He led us over to the hut. Inside, the casualties lay on the floor or were propped against the wall. Tom was slumped just by the door. He stared up at us and smiled and waved in recognition, but his speech was a blurred, morphine-fuelled stream of incoherence.

The water canteen he had been carrying on his hip had been shattered but it had saved his leg and maybe his life. There were messy wounds where shards of metal had been forced into his thigh, but the bones were not broken.

Some of the other casualties had horrific wounds, but Layla moved among them, fast but purposeful, showing no trace of panic as she assessed them. 'This one will wait. This one now.'

'What's our next move?' I said to Grizz, who had been talking on the satcoms while Layla was working.

'We must get the heli to the airport, load up as much ammo as we can carry and get back out to Bohara fast. It's still under attack.'

We loaded Tom and the worst of the wounded into the back

of the Huey. Grizz once more manned the door gun.

'You can sit in the front,' I said to Layla. 'The copilot won't be needing the seat and you're as safe there as anywhere.'

I called the tower at the airport, making sure they were aware that the incoming helicopter was friendly. 'This is Decisive Measures helicopter Grizzly One, flying from Sierra Leone Defences Force Camp Seventeen, seeking clearance to land.'

'Come on in, Grizzly One,' a laconic voice replied. 'You've got the place to yourself.'

We lifted off. I kept the Huey climbing to 5,000 feet, then banked towards Freetown. As we approached the airport I could see a transport aircraft with Nigerian markings unloading near the runway.

We landed and I helped Grizz and Layla unload the casualties. The most seriously injured were taken away in a rattletrap ambulance emblazoned with the Medicaid International logo; the less seriously wounded, Tom included, were seated on the ground.

Tom still looked spaced out. 'Will he be fit to fly?' I said.

Layla frowned. 'His leg is no problem; it's only a flesh wound. But he needs a few hours to get the morphine out of his system. Four hours absolute minimum, OK?'

I nodded then turned away to help Grizz.

We unlocked one of the bunkers and began loading boxes of ammunition, grenades and RPG rounds into the cab of the heli, stacking them roof-high and lashing them to the sides with webbing.

'What about Layla?' I said, as we worked.

'What about her? She comes with us.'

'It's too dangerous,' I said.

'It's too bloody dangerous everywhere these days. Besides, she's needed; they've taken casualties.'

WE WAITED FOR DUSK and the cover of darkness before taking off. Soon, it was a moonless night. The mountains rising to the north of us were blacker even than the night sky and the distant river winding beneath the canopy of the forest gleamed like dull pewter.

The airfield was blacked out and the only light was the faint glow of the instruments, but the darkness would give us some protection from rebel ground fire, and with night-vision goggles I could have flown the Huey down a coal mine at midnight.

Tom limped over to the Huey and climbed into the cockpit. I glanced behind into the cab. Grizz was stationed by the open door, squatting behind the mini-gun. Layla was precariously perched among the ammunition boxes. If we encountered ground fire and rounds went through the cab . . . I shook that thought off.

Just before I started the engines I shot a sideways glance at Tom. 'Are you really all right to take over control if you have to?' I said.

'No problem. Get on with it.' The waspish note in his voice gave me more reassurance than his words.

I fired the engines, grabbed the rotor brake and pushed the lever forward into flight idle. The drooping rotors creaked into life. The *whock-whock-whock* as they began to turn accelerated into a blur of noise and motion.

I pulled the night-vision goggles down over my eyes and switched them on. There was a faint electronic whine and the dark landscape turned green before my eyes, sparkling into life. The course of the river shone like a ribbon of light and the starlight flickered from the rotors like sparks of green fire.

I pressed the intercom. 'Here we go. Hold on, it's going to be a bumpy ride.'

I raised the collective and the Huey rose into the air. I held it at 100 feet as I got clearance from the tower and radioed ahead to Bohara. 'We're on our way. ETA twenty fifteen hours. Over.'

The reply was masked by static. 'The sooner the better.' I could hear the sounds of gunfire punctuating his words.

I put the Huey into a gradual descent. The changing air pressure in my ears told me we were descending without even having to look at the gauges or out through the canopy.

I waited until the altimeter hit fifty feet, then levelled. Still accelerating, we thundered eastwards into the night, rising and falling in response to my green-tinged vision of the unfolding terrain. I pushed us up to clear a ridge, then down again in a gut-loosening plummet to a valley floor, and rising once more to the next ridge. As I moved the controls, I gave a running commentary to Grizz and Layla in the back to help them brace themselves for the next lurch as the Huey swooped and soared, twisted and turned.

There had been no ground fire so far. I tried to imagine the unseen groups of rebel soldiers in the darkness ahead. They would have little warning of our approach, only a distant rumble of engines, swelling rapidly to a deafening clamour. There would be a storm of wind from the rotors and an unlit shape, black as a bat, flashing overhead. By the time they brought their weapons to bear, it would be too late.

We had been climbing steadily for some time to clear the last major ridge separating us from Bohara. As we neared the summit, the first starfires of shots pierced the darkness below us. I felt sweat start to my brow and gripped the controls even tighter. We cleared the ridge and lurched downwards in a sickening fall. I thumbed the radio. 'Bohara, this is Grizzly One. We are on approach now, taking incoming fire.'

I switched my gaze forward, looking for the signal from the unlit base. Then in the distance I saw a single square of beads of light begin to glow in the enveloping velvet blackness.

The ground fire was increasing in intensity now and I pushed down towards the rocky moonscape created by the mines.

As we approached Bohara, a blizzard of rounds filled the air and arcs of tracer seared upwards. Heavy-calibre tracer could cut through the heli's armoured skin like paper. I tried to ignore the stabbing streaks of red and orange light reaching up towards us. It seemed impossible that anything could fly through that inferno and not be carved into pieces. I jerked the heli left and right and sent it rising and falling, trying to unsettle the rebels' aim.

I looked ahead. A line of fierce red tracer slashed through the sky ahead of us. If we held our course, flying straight into a curtain of fire, we would be shot down.

I pulled an abrupt turn, swinging through 360 degrees in barely more than the Huey's own length. I heard a cry of surprise from Grizz in the back and a rattle as an ammunition box broke loose from its ties.

I held my breath, then saw the tracer exploding harmlessly behind us. It snapped off for a few moments, then reappeared, again slicing though the sky to overtake us. I pulled the same manoeuvre. Once more the tracer whipped past us and disappeared in our wake.

The compound lights had been extinguished after that one brief showing but one of the mercenaries was guiding me in using a torch with tape across the glass to leave only a thin, faint lozenge of light glowing in the darkness. I pulled back the cyclic, banking to land.

'Ground speed fifty, altitude one hundred feet,' Tom said.

I stamped alternately on the rudder pedals, twitching the tail from side to side in the hope of throwing off the aim of the rebel gunners, but, as I prepared to land, the torrents of ground fire increased still further. A moment later a string of flares ignited. As they drifted slowly down, they lit up the compound and the heli.

'We can't land,' Tom said. 'Just ditch the ammo and let's get out of here.'

I began to argue but I knew he was right. I pushed the intercom. 'We're going for a rolling drop. Get ready and I'll count you in.'

The seconds crawled by as we cleared the fence line and reached the drop zone. 'Three . . . two . . . one . . . Drop!'

Grizz and Layla started pushing and kicking out the cases of ammunition as I kept the Huey creeping forward over the floor of the compound. We were dropping the cases from thirty feet and I saw one split open as it hit the ground, spilling rounds onto the dirt, but Grizz was already shouting, 'Load clear. Go! Go! Go!'

I rammed up the collective and, free of the heavy load, we bucked into the air. I nosed the Huey over hard as soon as we were clear of radio antennae and satellite dishes on the accommodation block. I kept us climbing fast, moving out of range, disappearing back into the blackness of the night.

I grabbed the intercom. 'Everyone OK back there?'

'A few more holes in the cab,' Grizz said, 'but none in us.'

We flew back to the airport, but returned to Bohara twice more during the night, each time dumping more ammunition into the compound and then disappearing as rounds buzzed around the cockpit like angry hornets. On the second trip we managed to get Layla safely to the ground so that she could treat the wounded.

Dawn was breaking as we flew back to Freetown Airport again. We reached the airfield and I saw a giant Hercules transport drawn up near the Decisive Measures compound.

As soon as we'd landed, we began checking over the Huey. There were a few more perforations in its metal skin and some nicks in the edges of the rotors, but no significant damage. We turned away from the Huey in time to see a field gun being unloaded from the Herc.

'That's ours,' Grizz said. 'Let's grab some breakfast and then get that gun up to Bohara.'

'We're a sitting target already without a two-ton pendulum hanging underneath us,' Tom said. 'Do they really need it?'

'Those weren't fireworks the rebels were throwing, Tom,' I said. 'Of course they need it.'

I studied him for a moment. I'd been trained by him at Finnington when I was beginning my air force career in helis, but that was all I knew of him. When I discovered we'd be flying together again, I had asked the air-force rumour mill for information about him.

It appeared that Tom was a moderate pilot with an unexceptional career. There were no black marks on his record, but there was a whisper about him. The guy had served for twenty years in the air force—a period including the Falklands War, the Gulf War and Kosovo—and yet somehow he had never been in combat. My informants tapped their noses and hinted at a lack of bottle.

On the back of thirty hours with virtually no sleep, we had now been flying for over twelve hours nonstop. Close to exhaustion, I was flying as if on automatic pilot, but there was no question of refusing to fly the mission, least of all when the guys at Bohara were taking incoming fire. I sensed a difference in Tom's attitude, however, and his state of mind was already beginning to worry me.

'That's the job, Tom,' I went on. 'They need it, we deliver it.'

'Even if it gets us killed?'

'That's why they pay us the money.'

Grizz looked up. 'Listen, Tom, you've got a hard job, but it's nowhere near as tough as the one the guys at Bohara are doing.' He gave Tom a look that contained little sympathy, and walked away.

Tom watched him go, then turned to face me. He held my gaze, his voice quavering with barely suppressed emotion. 'I didn't come here to die, Jack. I came to get my life back on track and give myself a breathing space, not get shot to pieces over some stinking jungle.' He paused and softened his tone. 'You're younger than me. Things look more clear-cut to you: there's right and wrong and not much else in between. And you fly—like all the young guys—as if the shoot-downs only happen to other people.' He gripped my arm tightly. 'Well, they don't, Jack. They happen to people just like you and me. My luck's run out. I've been hit already. The next one'll kill me.'

As gently as I could, I disengaged his hand from my arm. 'You copped a flesh wound in your leg, Tom, that's all. If your luck had run out it would have killed you.' I paused, trying to find words to rally him. 'We're both knackered and by the book we've flown too many hours already, but we're going to get the job done. In a few hours' time we'll be sitting with our feet up and a cold beer in our hands, laughing about this conversation. Now let's get some food and water and then get airborne.'

He turned away. I watched him limp towards a street vendor who had set up shop on the edge of the airfield selling bean soup, smoked fish and rice. The price had gone up fivefold since the news of the rebel attacks had broken and he would take payment only in dollars, but there was little choice: it was that or K-rations.

While we ate, Grizz shouted and cajoled his private army into preparing the field gun. It was an ancient 25-pounder.

'I didn't know you were an antiques collector, Grizz,' I said.

He grinned. 'We use what we can get, smart arse. It's British Army surplus, but it still works all right and it'll land a round on a target just as well as a modern artillery piece—maybe even better.'

As we talked, the others sweated to loop two thick wire cables beneath the gun and stack the boxes of shells into the heli. When all was ready, we refuelled the Huey and I fired up the engines to pick up the 25-pounder. I flew forward and a guy crouching near the gun reached up and swung four cables over the hook as I held the heli in the hover. Then I heard Grizz shout, 'Got it. Let's go.'

The rotors struggled to haul the load off the ground. But finally, engines groaning, we began to climb. The controls felt sluggish under the added load and the drag of the gun. I adjusted the controls with small, almost imperceptible movements, knowing the danger of beginning a pendulum swing in the load that would increase until it threw the heli out of flying trim.

The flight to Bohara seemed to take for ever. The weight of the 25-pounder dangling below the Huey made every manoeuvre ponderous, and I knew that when we came under heavy fire it would be impossible to fly the normal patterns of evasion. Any attempt to climb or descend too steeply would simply send us crashing to earth.

The one trick I could employ was to approach from an unexpected direction. It was one of the first things we were taught in combat training: never use the same approach path twice or the enemy will set up guns under it and cut you to pieces the next time you fly in.

Instead of the direct approach to Bohara from the west, I therefore circled south and east of the compound, coming in from the opposite direction to the one the rebels would be expecting.

The drop-off was still fraught with danger, however. With the field gun trailing below us we could not even approach at low level. Instead, I came in high and then dropped towards the compound in a dive that, because of the destabilising weight of the 25-pounder, was neither as tight nor as rapid as I would have wished.

The rebel gunners opened up with everything they had. I could see scores of muzzle flashes and moments later rounds began to clip the fuselage. More bullets struck sparks from the field gun below us and then ricocheted away.

Grizz and Tom talked me down as a hail of rounds rattled from the armoured underside of the Huey. One whined away from the metal frame of the Perspex canopy. The next one pierced it, punching twin holes in either side of the cockpit a few inches from our heads and showering us with fragments of Perspex that rattled against my visor. Tom's voice cracked as he tried to give me instructions, but Grizz remained imperturbable, his words interspersed with bursts from the mini-gun. The rebels' brightly coloured T-shirts made them highly visible targets.

'Left thirty feet,' Grizz said. 'Hold it there and descend.' At last, he gave the command. 'That's it. Hold it there. Release!'

'Release,' Tom said, the relief evident in his voice. The heli lurched upwards as he hit the button and the dead weight dropped away.

We had hovered for no more than a minute, but in that time we were riddled with fire. More rounds struck the rotors and ripped through the cab walls. As we returned fire, spent casings from the mini-guns cascaded down onto the tin roofs in the compound.

Grizz already had the cases of shells for the field gun poised at the edge of the deck. I nosed the heli forward another twenty yards, clear of the 25-pounder, and he began kicking them out. More and more rounds struck the fuselage of the Huey. It seemed impossible that none had yet pierced a vital area. At last I heard Grizz's voice on the intercom. 'Last one clear. Go! Go! Go!'

I piled on the power. Free at last of the massive load, the Huey shot upwards into the sanctuary of the skies.

CHAPTER 6

We returned safely to the airfield at Freetown, but my thoughts of rest proved optimistic. We were back in action at once. As well as the field gun, fresh reinforcements had arrived in the Herc. There was a group of black South African troops and their white NCOs, and a ragged-looking bunch of white mercenaries—German, Russian, French and South African—all with the hard-eyed look of men who had killed before and would do so again.

'Decisive Measures seem to be getting a lot less choosy about where their recruits come from,' I said.

Grizz shrugged. 'Needs must. Let's get moving.'

By now, the run to Bohara had become almost routine, a high-level approach, followed by a breakneck, low-level dash over the last few miles, dodging the ground fire. Each run added a few more holes to the Huey, but I'd begun to feel almost invulnerable. I was at one with the machine, sure of its responses as I pushed it to the limits, the rotors skimming the treetops. We flared and landed or went into the hover over the compound only for the few seconds it took to drop the load we were carrying before we were airborne again in a fog of dust.

This time we landed, keeping the rotors turning fast as the mercenaries dumped out their weapons and kit and jumped down. As they did so the landing zone erupted with hostile fire. I heard the crack and tick of rounds piercing the helicopter's steel skin and ripping through the Perspex canopy above my head.

The seconds crawled by as the soldiers dragged their equipment out. 'Come on,' Tom shouted. 'Come on, let's go.'

'We're waiting for Layla,' Grizz said.

She had been treating some wounded at the compound, but was now returning to Freetown. I saw her come sprinting from the fortified container building, ducking and weaving as she ran across the compound and dived into the cab.

It seemed an age before Grizz called, 'She's in. Go. Go. Go.'

Before he had finished speaking, I was climbing and banking away from the rebel fire, swinging away as dust and smoke obscured the battlefield behind us.

Among the lines of ineffectual small-arms fire, I suddenly saw a series of huge, vivid red starbursts ripping upwards, outlined for a fraction of a second against the backdrop of bare rock and forest and then soaring up across the blue sky towards us. For a moment I refused to believe the evidence of my eyes.

'That's antiaircraft fire,' Tom said. 'That ZFU they told—' His voice trailed away.

Sweat poured from my brow as I jerked and twisted the Huey around in a frantic pattern of evasion. The unseen gunner tracked us, and the fireballs drifted closer. I pulled a maximum break and the red fires blasted the empty sky where we had been heading only a few seconds before.

I pulled another gut-wrenching turn, then froze. Red fire burned a line through the sky towards us like an oxyacetylene torch cutting metal. It disappeared in the blinding glare of the sun, then reappeared as a red flash directly ahead of us.

Time seemed to stop, then there was a blast and a crash, and a blurring frenzy of light, noise and heat. The red flares were on the inside of the cab, punching up through the armoured floor and out through the roof. The line burned its way across the floor, up through Tom's seat and out through the back of the cab.

There was the stench of burning, and a snowstorm of metal, plastic, rubber and fabric flew around me. Tom twitched a little, and then settled into his seat as if dropping off to sleep, but from the corner of my eye, I saw a rich, red stain spread over his flying suit.

For a second every screen was blank. Then there was a blizzard of flashing lights and a rising cadence of shrieking alarms. The Huey gave a savage lurch and went into an accelerating spin. Tracer rounds, red earth, dark green vegetation and blue sky blurred into a continuous multicoloured stream flashing past the cockpit.

Agonisingly slowly, each movement a huge effort, I pulled the levers, throttling back, cutting the power and the torque in an effort to hold it level. The landscape came back into focus.

I nursed the failing helicopter towards a gash in the trees where some forest giant had collapsed. It was strictly too narrow for the rotors but we had zero options. I lined up the heli, setting the tail rotor directly along the length of the gap.

I took a deep breath. Modern craft were lighter, constructed from materials unknown when the Huey was built, but the sheer solidity of the old helicopter had some advantages. The main rotors were almost fifty feet from tip to tip and the ballast weights at the ends gave the heavy blades such inertia that they could slice through brush and small branches without damage.

I began to inch us down. The body of the heli dropped below the treetops. As it sank lower there was a noise like gunfire and a snowstorm of wood fragments flew through the air.

The noise and the blizzard of splinters increased as we dropped. The rotors made harder work of cutting their way through the thicker lower branches and we were still sixty feet above ground when they hit an immovable object—the spike of a broken branch as thick as my thigh. The blurring rotors froze in front of my eyes and then shattered, sending silver shards knifing through the air.

The Perspex cracked, and a fragment of rotor blade smashed through it like a machete. Its leading edge sliced through my harness and into my chest. The Huey hit the ground with a crash that drowned out the warning siren, and I blacked out.

WHEN I OPENED my eyes, fragments of leaf were fluttering down onto the crumpled cockpit and a fog of orange-brown dust hung around it. My head was pounding and there was a stabbing pain in my chest. I could hear the hiss of fluid dropping on hot metal and the clicking of the engine as it began to cool. There was no sound from the surrounding jungle; every bird and animal had been put to flight by the crash of the helicopter.

I shook off my flying glove and touched my chest. My hand came away dark and sticky with blood. Then I looked to my right. Tom lay motionless in the copilot's seat. His flying suit from chest to ankles was a sodden mass of blood, his face as grey as if it had been cast from clay. I shuddered and looked away.

I called to Layla and Grizz. There was silence. Panic rose inside me. I called again, twisting my head to look behind me, then winced as the knife-sharp fragment of rotor blade sliced deeper into my flesh. It had been stopped by the breastbone. Had it penetrated a couple of inches further, I would have been dead.

I heard Grizz mutter something and then Layla's hesitant reply. I almost cried with relief. 'Don't try and move for a moment. I'll get myself free and then help you.'

I undid my harness, then pulled myself as far back into my seat as I could. The broken rotor blade had a barbed edge and the skin on my chest caught and pulled. I stifled a cry of pain as it tore free, leaving a small gobbet of flesh impaled on the hook like fishing bait.

As I squeezed through the gap into the cab I heard the crack of gunfire. Grizz was already out of his seat, wrenching the mini-gun from its mounting.

'Get Layla out and make a break for it,' he said. 'I'll give you cover.' He handed me a grenade. 'Blow the tanks with this when you're ready to go. The diversion'll give us all a better chance.'

'Where do we wait for you?'

'You don't. We'll RV back at Bohara.'

'But Grizz—'

'Don't argue. Get going.' He loosed off a burst of fire into the forest, then jumped out and sprinted for cover on the far side of the clearing.

I turned to Layla. 'OK?'

She nodded. 'What about Tom?' She read the answer in my face.

I grabbed a rifle and as many clips as I could stuff into the pockets of my combat vest. Then I slid open the door on the far side of the cab, waited for a burst of gunfire from Grizz, and waved her away towards the undergrowth at the edge of the clearing. She ran fast, low to the ground, dodging and weaving. As she dropped into cover behind a rotting tree trunk, I swung out of the door. I stuck the grenade into the neck of the fuel tank, pulled the pin and sprinted away from the Huey, throwing myself into cover alongside Layla.

The grenade exploded, followed at once by an even more massive blast as the fuel tank detonated. A pillar of flame shot into the air and debris whistled over our heads. As the echo of the blast faded, I was on my feet, grabbing Layla's arm. 'Come on.'

We turned and ran into the forest. The firing began again almost at once, but no shots followed us as we crashed through the undergrowth. We ran on until the gunfire was only the faintest of echoes, then slowed to a walk. It was hard to navigate through the dense forest, but I tried to keep us on a northwesterly bearing.

'What do we do?' she said.

'I don't want to make directly for Bohara. If the rebels are pursuing us, that's the direction they'll assume we're taking. We'll aim to pass north of the compound and then approach from the east—though there's a high chance of getting lost in this maze.'

We moved on. The trees soon began to thin, with patches of cleared land hacked and burned out of the forest. Some were planted with crops, showing that a village was not far away.

We reached the edge of the forest and looked out over a broad valley. A river wound through it and I could see a village set in a sea of elephant grass, a cluster of huts made of crude wattle-and-daub walls and palm-thatched roofs supported on bush-pole rafters.

We moved through the chest-high grass and crept up a low ridge to peer down at the village. It seemed a picture of tranquillity. Women sat in the doorways of their huts as children played around them. A few scrawny hens scratched at the dust. The younger women were returning from the river bank carrying head-loads of water and clean washing.

We lay watching for some time. 'What do you think?' I said.

'I know these people,' Layla said. 'I think we're safe here.'

As I began to get to my feet, I heard a faint noise behind me and then a blow exploded against my temple. I staggered and collapsed to my knees. When I raised my head, shaking it to clear my blurred vision, I found myself facing a group of at least twenty men. I closed my eyes, cursing myself for my stupidity. Our headlong flight through the forest must have left a trail a blind man could have followed. We should have kept moving through the grasslands, rather than pausing here, allowing the rebels to overtake us.

Their hair was tangled into rough dreadlocks plaited with scraps of ribbon, thread and shards of broken mirror. Their eyes were bloodshot and their pupils like pinpricks. Most were little more than boys, but there was no mistaking the murderous look in their eyes.

Their leader, a bloated, brutish-looking veteran at least eighteen years old, stood watching as we were searched. My combat vest was ripped from my back and handed to him, together with my rifle and ammunition clips. He emptied my wallet, tucking my money into his pocket. My survival equipment was picked over, then distributed among his men. When he found the GPS navigating device, however, he put it on the ground and drove the butt of his rifle down on it.

We were pushed down the hillside towards the village and there were shouts of alarm as we were spotted by the villagers. People began to run, only to find more rebels advancing into the village on all sides. The men and boys who had been out working in the fields were dragged in a few minutes later and the whole population was herded together on the trampled earth at the heart of the village.

The rebel leader pushed Layla and me into a corner by one of the huts. Two rebel soldiers stood guard over us.

I touched Layla's hand. 'I'm sorry I got you into this.'

'You didn't. I got myself into it. If you make it out of here, Jack, go and see my parents for me, will you?' A tear trickled down her cheek. 'Tell them what happened and say that, though I wished it hadn't ended this way, I still didn't regret having come here.'

'You can tell them yourself, the next time you're home.'

She gave an impatient shake of her head.

'All right,' I said. 'I promise I will.'

She held my gaze a moment longer.

We fell silent and sat huddled together, frightened and alone as the rebels looted the village. Food and jugs of palm wine were brought out of the huts and passed from hand to hand, and they were soon drunk. They began to interrogate the villagers, but after a few minutes, they gave up even a show of interest in the answers. They began chanting and singing, stamping their feet, moving ever closer, crowding the villagers together. Pangas began to rise and fall, the sun glinting from the blades. Layla stifled a scream and buried her face in my shoulder as a bloodied man collapsed to the ground. Then the rebel leader severed his victim's head with three strokes of his panga. He impaled the head on a stick and thrust it towards us, jeering at the terror he saw written on our faces.

The slaughter went on until the village was full of dead. The smell of blood hung over it, sweet and sickly.

The boys were forced to become recruits. Each one was made to identify his parents and then ordered to kill them. If he refused, he was killed himself. But after this had happened three or four times the boys began killing their parents as soon as they were ordered to do so.

Tears running down our cheeks, we watched the surviving boys and young men, most too stunned even to cry, being marched away. Now only the girls and young women remained in the village. The leader stayed with the two rebels guarding us. The rest of them dragged the girls away, ripping off their clothes and holding them down as each soldier took his turn. It was like a soundtrack from hell, with cries, groans and screams coming from all sides.

The leader watched for a moment, a smile on his face, then turned towards us. His gaze switched from me to Layla as he licked his lips, his tongue darting out like a snake tasting the air.

He signalled to the other two to take my arms. As I strained against the two holding me, I felt sharp steel prick my throat and forced myself to remain still.

The leader moved round behind Layla, placing one hand on her hip. Clutching a panga in his other hand, he began to propel her towards one of the huts, thrusting his hips against her buttocks to push her forward.

As he reached the entrance he paused and called out to the two men guarding me. They gave a burst of harsh laughter. One of them propped the RPG he was carrying against the wall of the hut and held a blade against my neck. The other stood in front of me. His T-shirt was stained with blood, dirt and sweat and when he spoke he showed a mouthful of black and rotting teeth. He stretched out a hand and stroked my cheek, then said something to the other rebel. They both laughed again.

He took a knife from the sheath on his belt and pressed the point against my chin, forcing my head up. I felt a stab of pain and blood trickled down my neck. The knife point worked lower, tracing a line down my throat and chest. He cut off the buttons of my shirt one by one and then slid the knife down the waistband of my trousers.

Suddenly there was a terrible screaming from the hut where the rebel leader had taken Layla, so high-pitched it sounded as if no human voice could have made such a sound. Even my captors were momentarily nonplussed.

I gave up the last shreds of hope. Layla was dead. I would be next. Better to die fighting than humiliated and murdered. I tensed myself, poised to attack. I might at least get one of them before the other cut me to pieces.

Then I heard a footfall and a thin, sibilant sound, 'Sssst! Sssst!'

I looked up. The face of the rebel guarding me had become a red mask of blood. The sound came again, 'Sssst!'

There was a squeal like a slaughtered hog and the bulk of the other man crashed down on my back. Writhing to be free of his dead weight, I forced myself away from him and swung around. Then I saw his staring eyes and the gaping gash in his neck. Blood still spilled from it, but he was already dead.

I looked up. Layla stood there, her skirt ripped and stained. Blood dripped from the blade of the panga she held in her hand. She met my gaze, her eyes blank and hard, but as she looked down again at the bodies, her face crumpled and the panga dropped from her grip.

I hauled myself to my feet. 'We've got to get out of here,' I said, my voice cracking. 'Now.'

The rebel commander staggered into view, blood drenching his thighs, screaming and shouting. I looked round. The soldiers' weapons were still propped against the wall of the hut. I reached for a rifle, eased off the safety catch and took aim.

The shot hit him low and slightly left, ripping through the side of his abdomen. The force of the impact spun him round and his body jerked as I fired again and again. At last he dropped and lay still.

I dropped the rifle and stared at my hands. To pilots, war could sometimes seem an arcade game. Now I was mired in the bloody, terrifying, ground-level reality of the most brutal and vicious warfare that the mind of man could devise.

'Jack!' Layla's fingers were digging into my arm.

I looked up. A group of rebels was sprinting towards us, yelling and screaming. I reached for the rifle, then checked and picked up the RPG instead. I fumbled with it, pressed it into my shoulder, sighted and pulled the trigger. Nothing happened. I jerked it down, groped for the safety catch and then pulled it up again.

The lead rebel was no more than twenty yards away. As I sighted along the barrel I saw his face change as he spotted the RPG. Then I pulled the trigger. There was a roar and a blast. The rocket punched a hole through his guts and detonated against a rock a yard away from him. The shrapnel cut down all the other rebels within range, but the noise brought the rest of them swarming back into the centre of the village like hornets.

Smoke filled my lungs and I coughed. The wall of the hut was on fire, ignited by the back blast of the RPG. Half-blinded by smoke, I grabbed the panga, the rifle and a belt of ammunition, and pushed Layla away. We stumbled towards the forest, hearing the shouts of the rebels in our ears. The first shots whined around us.

As we reached the trees I turned to loose off a burst from the rifle. One rebel toppled but the others did not even falter in their pursuit. I turned again and we ran for our lives along the track, deeper and deeper into the forest.

We ran until I thought my lungs would burst, then I checked at a faint break in the wall of vegetation. We dived through it, then twisted round, spreading the foliage back across the gap. We flattened ourselves, worming our way down into the leaf litter of the forest floor, and lay still.

The wild beating of my heart drowned any sound of pursuit at first, but then I heard the slap of bare feet running towards us. The rebels loped into view, indifferent to their own safety, running steadily, confident of overhauling us. Through the screen of foliage I saw the face of the lead man, scanning the jungle for marks that might show where we had gone.

I dropped my head and lay still as they moved closer, though my flesh crept. The footsteps slowed. I held myself motionless, though every instinct screamed at me to run before it was too late.

The seconds dragged by. Then I heard the footsteps move on again down the track. I waited until the sounds had faded and my heart had stopped its pounding, and was about to raise my head when I caught a faint noise. I froze. The sound grew louder, a soft scuffing in the dust of the forest track.

The noise stopped. I saw a bare foot no more than a yard away. The hairs on my neck rose. Knowing that any movement, however slight, would give us away, I forced myself to remain motionless, gritting my teeth and offering silent prayers that the rebel would miss us and move on. There was nothing separating us from death but a single scrubby bush and a thin covering of leaf litter. I could feel a faint trembling in my arm, but could do nothing to stop it.

I heard the soft rustle of cloth and saw the foot move as he turned towards the other side of the track, but after a moment he turned back. An arm came into my view as he reached down and fingered a broken plant stem.

A voice broke the silence and I almost jumped out of my skin. He had spoken in the local language and, though I did not understand the words, his tone told me the game must be up. He had seen us and was telling us to come out.

I was tensing my muscles to ease myself up slowly enough to avoid alarming him and provoking a shot, when he was answered by another man behind him on the track.

There was a long silence, then an abrupt word of command and I heard again the faint scuffing noise and saw two pairs of feet moving away along the track.

I remained absolutely motionless, my heart still hammering in my chest until the calls of birds told me we were safe, for the moment at least. I rose slowly, peered along the empty track, then took Layla's arm and led her deeper into the jungle.

CHAPTER 7

We kept walking for another hour before I felt it was safe enough to pause. We stopped at the bank of a forest stream and Layla sank to the ground at once. Her face was bruised and cut and her hair was matted with blood. I took off my tattered shirt, rinsed the sweat and dirt from it and then gently cleaned her face. As I reached over to dab at a cut over her eye, I put a hand on her arm to steady myself. She recoiled and pulled away from me at once.

'Are you all right?' I said.

She didn't reply. Her eyes remained fixed on mine, but she seemed to be staring straight through me.

'Did he—' I checked and changed the question. 'How did you get away from him?'

Her voice was harsh and flat. 'I don't want to talk about it and if we get out of this alive, I never want anyone else to know what happened back there in that village.'

I saw her eyes fill with tears and tried to cradle her head against my shoulder, but she pushed me away, fury in her face. She stood up and walked off, turning her back to me, but I saw her body racked with sobs. I waited in silence until she had grown quiet again.

'Do you want to wash yourself?' I said. 'I'll keep watch.'

She shivered, as if waking from a nightmare, then turned her tear-stained face towards me. 'I'd like that, thanks.'

I moved away a few more yards and stood with my back to her as she stripped off and bathed herself in the stream water.

When she had finished, we changed places. I took off my clothes, crouched on the bank and began washing myself. I scooped up handfuls of sand from the bed of the stream and scoured myself with it. I felt I could have washed myself for a week and still not got clean.

'What do we do?' Layla said, after I'd pulled my clothes back on.

'I don't know. I thought we might make Bohara, but with no map and no GPS, I think our only hope is to make for Freetown.'

'But we can't cross the country on foot. And how will we navigate?'

'The river was north of us, wasn't it? All we can do is use the sun to navigate and make our way north until we find the river.'

'And then?'

'Try to steal a boat, I suppose.'

I moved a few paces upstream and then took a rough bearing from the sunlight filtering through the forest canopy.

The twists and turns we had to make around the impenetrable stands of trees and dense undergrowth made our progress slow, and it was easy to get disorientated. The direction of the sun was often obscured by the tree cover.

The foliage frequently reduced visibility to no more than five yards, but my other senses seemed heightened in compensation. I paused every few steps to listen for the sound of movement or the distress cries of birds, and I sniffed the faint breeze for any human trace.

At length I heard a faint sound. It grew into the steady ripple of moving water. I caught a glint through the undergrowth and, parting the leaves, looked out on a broad, slow-moving river.

We tracked the river westwards. Shortly before sunset I saw a dark shape on the far bank. As we drew closer, the shape resolved itself into the mud walls and rough thatch of a ferryman's hut.

A battered craft was tied up at the water's edge on the far side and a wire cable ran from bank to bank, sagging into the river in the middle. It was secured at the base of thick posts driven into the soil on either bank. The cable passed through steel eyes at each end of the boat; the ferryman could punt across the river, guided by the cable.

We lay down to wait for full darkness.

Half an hour after the faint glow of a candle or lantern in the building had been extinguished, I left Layla in our hiding place and crawled forward through the vegetation. I got to my feet next to the post securing the cable and gave the rusting wire an experimental pull. The boat remained motionless, but the protesting squeal of rusty metal penetrated the night.

I dropped to the ground. A second later the hut door opened and I saw the outline of a rebel soldier, the barrel of his gun black against the sky. He made a desultory search around the hut, but he found nothing and moments later I heard the bang of the door.

I waited ten minutes, then knotted the carrying loop of my rifle, clenched the strap in my teeth and lowered myself into the water. I began to haul myself along the cable, hand over hand, my head tilted back to help keep the rifle free of the water.

Dark shapes sent my heart racing as they swirled past me. They were only branches but, to my frightened eyes in the gloom of the night, each looked like a water snake or an alligator.

My arms were aching with the effort and I began to shiver with cold. I forced myself on again, but had hardly moved when a log, carried on the current, crashed into my shoulder. I gasped with shock.

Just as I felt I could go no further and my numbed fingers were beginning to lose their grip on the cable, my right hand bumped against something hard. The shallow, metal, flat-bottomed ferry-boat was no more than ten feet long and less than half that in width. I worked my way alongside it and crawled out onto the bank. I lay gasping on the mud, waiting for my strength to return.

I stared towards the hut, straining my ears for any sound, then began to work on the rotting post that held the steel cable. I heaved at it with all my strength, but it barely moved.

I saw the pale disc of Layla's face watching me from the far bank. I had to release the boat. It was our only hope. I knew what I had to do—for her as well as for me.

I crouched down behind the ferryboat no more than five yards from the hut and set the rifle on automatic. I aimed six inches above the ground and then raked the hut from left to right and right to left. I heard a scream. Then, a rebel trailing one leg behind him lurched through the door of the hut, shooting without aiming as he stumbled towards the boat where I lay hidden. I fired another burst. The impacts hurled him back against the wall of the hut and he slumped to the ground and lay still. I put another burst into the hut to be sure, then I stepped out of cover and moved to the doorway.

In the faint glow of the embers from their dying fire, I could see another body lying inside the hut. This was no soldier. The ferry-man had been unarmed and unprotected, wearing only shorts and a faded T-shirt. The shots I had fired had hit him in the head, chest and thigh as he lay asleep. The burning taste of bile was in my throat as a wave of shame swept over me.

I searched the hut, aware that every second was now vital. The noise of the gunfire would have been heard for miles up and down the river, and even now a rebel patrol might be moving to investigate.

I had hoped to find an axe or a shovel but there was only a panga. I took it outside.

I ran to the dead soldier, intending to use his rifle as a crowbar, but as I picked it up I saw a grenade hanging from his belt. I hacked at the post with the panga until I had carved out a rough hollow beneath the cable. Then I forced the grenade into it, pulled the pin and sprinted for the cover of the boat. There was a flash and a blast and I heard shrapnel rattle against the metal hull.

I ran back to the post. Most of the cable had been shredded but a few strands still held. I picked up the panga and hacked at them.

There was a crack as the last strand snapped. The ferryboat began to drift away from the bank. I ran down the slippery mud bank and half jumped, half dived for the boat, just managing to catch the gunwale as it swirled away on the current. I dragged myself up and over the side and fell onto the bottom boards. Still attached to the cable on the far bank, the boat swung in a pendulum curve out across the water, past the midpoint of the river and in towards the far bank. Then the cable tautened and the boat held station, some twenty yards from the water's edge.

I called to Layla but she was already racing along the bank towards me. As she began wading out towards the boat, I heard a scraping sound and then a twang as the cable pulled free of the guidehole in the stern. The end snaked past me. It was checked for a moment by the guidehole on the bow of the boat, then it pulled clear and fell away with a splash.

Layla lunged for the gunwale as the boat gathered speed, and I grabbed her arm and dragged her bodily into the boat. We lay flat, gasping with exertion, as our craft moved away downstream.

We were soon well downriver of the ferryman's hut, carried headlong by the rip of the current. Within seconds the fear of striking a rock in the darkness pushed me upright. There was no rudder, only a long punt pole lying in the bottom of the boat. I trailed it over the stern and used it as a makeshift rudder. Eventually, when we encountered a long stretch of rapids, I tried to steer for the bank, but the strength of the current was too great and we were carried sideways towards the rocks. The noise of the rapids reverberated around us as we entered a steep ravine, its walls smoothed and scoured by the force of rainy season floods. I could barely steer.

I shipped the punt pole, and Layla and I clung to the sides of the boat with both hands as it barrelled through the water, cannoning off the flanks of the rocks in its path. Finally our luck ran out. The boat was driven headlong onto a massive rock in the centre of the channel. I felt a bone-jarring shock and was thrown out.

As it was swept away into the darkness, I heard Layla scream, then I was fighting for my life, floundering and only just keeping my head above water. The rapids hurled me onwards. I was bumped and battered so hard from rock to rock that I could hardly draw breath. My fingers clawed for grip on the smooth, slimy rocks but each time I was dragged away again. I could see nothing in the darkness and hear nothing but the thunder of the water echoing from the bare rock walls of the gorge. It was as much as I could manage to gulp in a fresh mouthful of air before the next surge of water swept over my face and whirled me away again downstream.

The thunder of the rapids seemed to fade, then the waters again closed over my head and blackness enveloped me.

I regained consciousness, choking and retching. I could feel water still lapping round my legs but there was gritty sand against my cheek. Then strong hands pressed down on my chest and a fresh spasm of coughing shook me as more water poured from my mouth.

I opened my eyes. Layla sat astride me. When she saw me looking at her, she hugged me and kissed my face. 'Thank God. I thought I'd lost you.'

I raised my head a little. The boat was drawn up on the narrow beach a few feet away. Upstream to my right, I could make out the rapids spilling out of the entrance to the canyon. The river flowed fast and silent past the beach where I lay. I pushed myself up to a sitting position and took a few deep breaths. 'Let's get out of here.'

In the grey light of approaching dawn, we clambered back into the boat and Layla pushed off with the pole. We slipped downstream, fast at first, but as we drifted farther from the rapids, the river began to meander on a leisurely course across the marshlands that separated us from the coast.

We drifted with the current, peering into the water, trying to discern the telltale eddies troubling the surface as the river passed over shallows and swirled around sandbars and sunken rocks. Three times we had to beach the boat and half drag, half carry it over the shallows to the next navigable stretch.

The river bank was now barely a foot above the surface of the water. We passed islands from which palm trees grew. Herons stalked through the shallows, stabbing at the black mud with their beaks.

The river divided and then split again and, as the sky lightened, we found ourselves drifting through a series of progressively narrower and more sluggish waterways, with the mangroves growing so close around us that they scraped the sides of the boat.

Finally we came to a mud flat and a slight break in the wall of mangroves. As I stared at the mud in the dawn light, I saw a series of footprints leading away from the water. Whatever the dangers it might herald, it at least promised a way out of the swamps. We dragged the boat out of the water and began to follow the trail. Stumbling over submerged roots, we worked our way at snail's pace through the thickets, trying to steer a course between the main channel of the river and the first signs of habitation—the settlements fringing the shore.

As we plodded on, exhausted and weak from hunger, the path became better defined. Palm logs were laid as bridges over the creeks and small rivers, and among the mangroves were patches of paddy fields studded with vivid green rice shoots.

At last the mangroves began to thin and the track started to open out ahead of us. After the gloom of the swamp, I had to shield my eyes from the morning light.

The tide was low and the river channel was flanked by broad expanses of glistening mud. Boats were drawn up on the opposite bank. The near bank was empty. A steep hillside half a mile ahead hid Freetown from us, but I could see smoke rising from its shantytown.

'If we can get past here we should be safe,' I said.

'Always assuming the rebels haven't attacked the capital while we've been making our way back here,' Layla said.

'Let's assume the worst but hope for the best,' I said.

We struck out along the bank. It was slow going, skirting treacherous stretches of mud that sucked at our legs like quicksand, and picking our way over rotting logs and past shacks and shanties that were perched just above the high-water mark.

Suddenly a figure appeared no more than thirty yards in front of us. We dropped to the ground and froze. A woman walked out to the edge of the river, her footprints black against the wet mud. She filled a cooking pot with water and then returned the way she had come.

We moved on again, our progress slower and slower as more people appeared at the river's edge to wash or fetch water. As we passed the mouth of a filthy street lined with mean shacks, a dog barked at us and then slunk away between two huts.

My heart was in my mouth. If the alarm was raised we would quickly be surrounded by hundreds of people. I had seen some of the inhabitants of the shantytown at work on the way in from the airport the day I had arrived in Sierra Leone. They might hand us over to the rebels, or they might rob and murder us themselves.

I was torn between the need to avoid rousing the people and a wave of panic that made me want to run headlong for the mouth of the river and the relative safety of the beaches that lay beyond.

As we rounded a bend we came face to face with a woman carrying a bucket of water on her head. She froze for a moment, her jaw dropping with astonishment at seeing us there. Then she dropped the bucket and turned and ran.

Layla laid a restraining hand on my arm. 'There's nothing we can do,' she said. 'Let's just keep moving.'

Past the last, ragged fringes of the shantytown the mud began to give way to yellow sand, speckled with grey grass stalks. I heard the roar of breakers and we hurried on, along a beach alive with small crabs. The fronds of the ragged palms fringing the sands rustled overhead like dry brown paper.

CHAPTER 8

We worked our way along the deserted beach until we were almost directly behind our hotel. Then we crawled forward through the dune grass and peered out at the building and the city beyond.

My head was pounding. I ran my tongue over my dry, cracked lips. We needed water. I felt an overpowering urge to run straight to the hotel, but I fought it down. We had been out of touch for days. Had a rebel offensive been launched against the capital, we could be heading straight into a deathtrap.

We lay in hiding, watching and waiting. The streets were almost deserted—a worrying sign that something was wrong—and yet there was a disarming air of normality about the few people and vehicles we did see moving about. It was the arrival of a delivery van at the rear of the hotel that led to my next movements. The scent of warm bread wafting to us on the breeze set the saliva flowing in my mouth and my stomach rumbled in anticipation.

'Come on,' I said, getting to my feet. 'It's OK, I'm sure of it.' We walked down the slope from the dunes, crossed the concrete access road and entered the building.

There was a handful of people in the lobby. None carried weapons and I felt the tension ebbing from me. The hotel guests lapsed into a stunned silence as we walked in. I caught a glimpse of our reflections in a mirror and could see why. Two mud-stained, wild-eyed, near skeletons stared back.

The Lebanese owner peered at me from behind the reception desk, trying to identify the mud-covered stranger in front of him.

'We need water,' I said. 'And food. And then a shower and a bed.'

He continued to stare at me, uncertainty written on his face.

I tried again. 'We were staying here a few days ago. I'm Jack Griffiths. I'm with Decisive Measures.'

His face now wreathed in smiles, he clapped his hands to summon his staff. 'Mr Griffiths, of course. I will have your room prepared at once. Perhaps you would prefer to shower before you eat.'

I shook my head. 'Water and bread now.'

He barked an order at a slouching waiter, then ushered us to the dining room. I felt my knees buckle and had to slump in a chair before I fell. The waiter brought a jug of water and I gulped some down, then fell on the basket of naan bread he proffered.

Layla laid a warning hand on my arm. 'Take it easy,' she said. 'Eat and drink a little, then wait before you swallow some more. Give your body time.' She sipped at her water as she spoke, then took a small mouthful of bread.

We sat there for half an hour, hardly speaking a word, just eating, drinking and smiling at each other. At length, I pushed back my chair and got unsteadily to my feet. 'I've got to have a shower but I think I'm too hyper to sleep.'

She nodded. 'Me too. Let's get away from these people, though.'

As we walked through the lobby, I stopped at the desk and picked up the phone, planning to call the Decisive Measures HQ in the hope of getting word on the situation at Bohara. The line was dead. The owner spread his hands. 'Out of order, I'm afraid. The phones seem to be out all over the capital.'

I tried to read his expression. 'Is everything quiet here?'

He gave a flustered smile. 'It's very quiet. Not many guests.'

'That's not what I meant. I was talking about the rebels.'

'There is fighting in the mountains, but they will not dare attack Freetown.' He glanced around the lobby, measuring the effect of his words on the hotel guests, then leaned over the counter and lowered his voice. 'There are rumours, though. People are leaving the city.'

'What rumours? Which people?'

'The President is unpopular. The army has not been paid. The President's son flew to Guinea yesterday.' He tapped his nose. 'They say the aircraft that took him has returned to await its next passenger.'

'We'll get a better idea later,' I said to Layla as we walked to the stairs. 'If the phones are still knackered I'll go to the High Commission and contact Decisive Measures from there.'

'And I'll go to Medicaid International,' she said. 'I should have reported in already, they'll be worried about me.'

'To hell with it,' I said. 'Let's catch up on the world later on.

We've earned a bit of rest after what we've been through.'

When we reached the first floor, we stood in silence on the landing, looking at each other. I ached to take her to my room, crush her to me and bury myself in her body, then sleep with our arms wrapped around each other, cut off from whatever awaited us. But still I hesitated, unsure of her response. 'Would— Do you—' I began at last.

She stood on tiptoe, took my face in her cool hands and kissed me, but when she felt me responding, she stepped back. 'I'm sorry,' she said. 'I can't, not yet. It's too soon. But I don't want to be on my own. Can we just . . . ?'

For answer, I put my arm round her waist, supporting her as we shambled away down the corridor to my room.

The rifle I had left behind a week before was still propped in a corner down the side of a wardrobe. I sat down on the edge of the bed. 'You shower first.'

She emerged twenty minutes later, her hair damp and her body wrapped in a threadbare towel, barely long enough to cover her. I saw the marks of lacerations and dark, purpling bruises on her thighs and felt anger burning in me. As she looked towards me I averted my gaze, as if I'd been caught spying on her.

I stood under the trickling shower, soaping my hair and body until the dirt had been washed away. I checked myself in the bathroom mirror and was shocked at my condition. There were black, sunken hollows under my eyes, I had lost several pounds in weight and my skin was a mass of abrasions, bruises and insect bites.

I pulled on some clean clothes and walked through to the bedroom. Layla was lying on the bed covered by the sheet. She held out her arms to me. 'Come and hold me while we talk.'

I lay next to her, feeling the unaccustomed softness of the bed beneath me, and very aware of the warmth of her body against mine.

'There's something I have to ask you,' Layla began. 'The last time we were in this hotel, you spent most of the evening avoiding telling me why you were in Sierra Leone. After all we've been through, do you feel ready to tell me yet why an otherwise apparently sane and decent human being would want to become a mercenary here?'

'All right.' I hesitated. I didn't want to lie to her but I was afraid of what she might think if I told her the truth. 'There was an operation in Kosovo,' I said at last. 'It went badly wrong.'

'Tell me about it. Only if you want to, of course, it's none of my business, but . . .' Her voice trailed away.

I held her gaze. 'No, I want to tell you. It was when the Serbs were really tearing the country apart. We were flying nonstop missions looking for targets—tanks, artillery, anything that presented itself. Then base picked up intelligence on some suspected hostiles. My wingman and I were sent to investigate. We made a few passes over the area and I glimpsed some vehicles hidden in the woods. I made another pass, then another, trying to decide. I was also hoping to draw some fire that would have confirmed them as hostile.

'My wingman said they were definitely hostile, but I still wasn't sure. I went round again, put the heli into the hover near the wood and then I saw people sprinting for the vehicles. I hesitated a little longer, then I made up my mind. We attacked. We flew in at low level and I fired my rocket pods at the vehicles. I was circling for another attack when I saw a figure running out of the trees. It was a woman wearing a long black skirt. She was on fire. She raised her arms above her head as if she were pleading with me. Then she fell to the ground.' Tears were now streaming down my face. 'She'd managed to escape from the Serbs. A group of her people were hiding in the woods with their farm trucks and tractors and carts. If the Serbs had found them, the men would have been killed and the women raped. But they'd survived. The Serbs had gone. Then I killed them.'

Layla didn't reply, but she reached up and stroked my face as I got myself under some sort of control.

'I'm sorry,' I said. 'I've never told anyone about that before.'

We lay in silence for some time. 'I used to dream that one day I would be famous,' Layla said. She smiled. 'But the older I get, the more I realise that life is about really small things. If we can do a little bit more good than harm while we're passing through, that's probably about as good as it gets for most people.'

'In that case, my personal ledger is way out of balance,' I said.

She gripped my arm, her fingers digging into my flesh, trying to impress upon me the importance of what she was saying. 'Then that's all the more reason to start balancing the books now. You can't change the past, but you can change the future. You don't want to be looking back in old age and still seeing that woman in Kosovo.'

She fell silent, studying my face, and when she spoke again her voice was little more than a whisper. 'I killed a child once. It was when I was training as a doctor. I was a houseman, a junior doctor. I was dog-tired at the end of a very long shift, but of course that's no excuse. Somehow—I don't know how, I knew what the right dose should be—I gave the baby three times the normal dose of a drug. Her heart stopped. I killed her.'

'But you've saved hundreds of others since.'

'I killed that one. When I close my eyes I can still see her little crumpled figure in the cot and her parents turning to look at me and asking, "Why? What happened?" And do you know what? I didn't even have the guts to admit what I had done.' She fell silent again, staring past me. 'So, we've both had to learn to live with mistakes,' she said eventually. 'I can understand why you left the air force, but that still doesn't explain why you came to Sierra Leone.'

'I didn't ever want to be in a position where I could get it so terribly, horribly wrong again. But flying helicopters is what I do. There's no civilian work; there are thirty pilots for every job that's going. I thought this would be a safe option; not many people want this kind of posting, but it suited me.'

She gave me a gentle smile. 'If the reasons you joined the air force were good ones, what happened in Kosovo shouldn't negate them. It was a tragic accident, but you can't just run away from it.' She paused. 'I ducked my responsibilities to the family of that dead girl and I'll never forgive myself for that, but I didn't give up medicine because of it. I know that nothing I can ever do will end the heartbreak her parents must feel. All I can do is try to help other sick children and make sure I never make such a terrible mistake again.' She held my gaze as she spoke. 'You've got to do the same kind of thing, Jack. You can't just sit on the sidelines, least of all in Sierra Leone. If you're here at all, you're either part of the problem or part of the solution.' She fell silent. 'I'm sorry. I'm a fine one to lecture you, aren't I? I spend my life butting my head against every obstacle that presents itself.'

'We make a good team then,' I said. 'We cancel out some of each other's weaknesses.'

She gave me a long, thoughtful look. 'That's one way of looking at it. But what if we cancel out each other's strengths instead?'

'If we did, we wouldn't be having this conversation now. We'd be lying dead back there in that jungle somewhere.'

The light was fading now. She kissed me, then sat up. 'I'm going back to my room,' she said. 'I need to sleep now.'

'Sleep here,' I said.

She shook her head. 'I need to be alone for a while to think things through.' She held on to my hand for a moment, then stood up.

I watched her all the way to her door and as it closed behind her, I whispered, 'I love you,' to the empty corridor.

Despite my exhaustion, it was a long time before I fell asleep. When I did, I was soon in the grip of the familiar nightmare: the thunder of guns, the burning figure, and the crushing feelings of helplessness and guilt. Then, finally, I was awake, with the sound of explosions and gunfire in my ears. This was no dream.

I rolled off the bed onto the floor, then crawled to the window and peered out. Dawn had not yet broken, but I could see the flash of explosions and the lurid glare of flames.

I picked up the rifle. As I felt my way along the darkened corridor towards Layla's room, I heard a door open and saw her silhouetted in the flash of another explosion in the heart of the city. I called her name and we clung to each other.

'I was just coming to find you,' she said, her voice shaking with fear. 'What do we do?'

'Try to find out what's going on.'

'Are we safe in the hotel?'

'I guess so, as safe as anywhere. If we go charging out into the night, we're just putting ourselves in greater danger. We'll stay here until we know what's happening.'

We groped our way to the stairs and went down to the lobby. There was no one to be seen. The hotel staff and, more worryingly, the security guards paid to protect the building had obviously reached their own conclusions about the shooting. All had fled.

The owner was not in evidence, but his office was unlocked. I tried to dial the British High Commission, but the lines were still dead. There was a transistor radio on the desk, but when I turned it on I heard only the hiss of static from the local channels. It was another ominous sign.

I tuned the radio to the BBC World Service instead. We had to endure forty minutes of magazine programmes before the next news bulletin. We were the lead item: 'Reports are coming in of an attempted coup in Sierra Leone. Sections of the armed forces have mutinied and made simultaneous attacks on the airport, the radio station and Government House in the capital, Freetown. There are unconfirmed reports of killing and looting in the capital . . .'

I returned to the local channel. A scratched recording of martial music was playing, but a few minutes later it was replaced by a rebel spokesman. He announced that the government and 'key installations' were already in rebel hands and proclaimed an immediate curfew, breaches of which would be punished by death. He warned 'foreign troops not to get involved with the internal affairs of the new republic of Sierra Leone'.

I forced a smile. 'I guess that means me and the rest of the boys.'

'What do we do now?'

'We need to know a bit more about what's going on. Meanwhile we stay put. We'd be safest from the firing somewhere near the heart of the building, but I guess we'll be better off up where we can see what's happening. If the rebels decide to storm the hotel, we need enough warning to be able to make a break for it. I don't fancy our chances'—I held her gaze—'especially yours—if they find us here.'

We went back to the lobby. The handful of other residents had congregated there. They had dressed in haste and now stood debating what to do. Some were for making a dash for the airport at once; others preferred to wait for daylight.

The hotel owner had appeared and was fussing around the group, imploring them not to panic, to wait to see what daylight brought. It was hard to tell if his concern for them was personal or financial.

We left them and went down to the kitchens for some food and water, then up to the first floor. The door to the corner suite was locked, but I kicked it open. The suite had windows looking south along the beach road where some of the expatriate houses were, and east, down the hill to the city centre. We drew the curtains, leaving only a chink through which we could see out, then we sat back to watch and wait, huddled together, her head resting on my arm.

Explosions continued to light up the night and there were regular, sustained bursts of small-arms fire.

Just before dawn, two vehicles crammed with people stormed out of the hotel car park and away down the hill. The group advocating a break for the airport had obviously won the day.

We tracked the taillights of the cars until they disappeared from sight. Shortly afterwards there was a prolonged burst of gunfire from the direction they had taken. Our eyes met, but neither of us spoke, though I felt Layla shaking as she cried soundlessly.

The first light of dawn revealed a pall of grey smoke hanging over the city. Peering out through binoculars from our hiding place, I saw rebel soldiers advancing along the road. Most wore sunglasses, T-shirts and stolen clothes piled layer upon layer over their threadbare fatigues. Like the rebels we'd encountered before, they had mirror fragments and bits of multicoloured plastic woven into their hair.

As they moved through the streets, they searched each building by shooting wildly into it. Then the looting began. The streets lower down the hill were soon strewn with debris and smashed glass.

'Where are the government troops?' I asked.

'Don't hold your breath. They defected to the rebels en masse in the last uprising. They're on whichever side they think will win.'

From the windows facing the beach road, I could see the homes of expatriates being stripped. The Lebanese traders were the most vulnerable targets. Those who had not taken the precaution of buying the protection of the rebel leaders—and perhaps even some who had—were robbed of everything. Most people had already fled or gone into hiding. The terrible screams we could hear echoing through the deserted streets told of the fate many others were suffering.

At noon, the rebels began to advance towards the hotel.

'Come on,' I said. 'If we stay, we're finished. Let's get out of here.'

'To where?'

I shrugged. 'The High Commission.'

She gave me a doubtful look. 'I think our best destination is the Medicaid International compound. I'll be needed there anyway. There'll be a lot of wounded. And whatever else the rebels are destroying, I'm sure they won't attack there.'

'I wish I shared your confidence,' I said. 'The High Commission has well-armed guards to protect it. The rebels are likely to leave it alone because they won't want to provoke a direct intervention by British troops. It's a much safer bet.'

'For you maybe, but I have to reach Medicaid International. I'm a medic, Jack, I'm needed there.'

We ran down to the lobby. Only the owner remained, sobbing and wringing his hands. He ran to us and seized my arm. 'What will I do?' he said. 'Please bring help, bring soldiers before it is too late.'

I gently disengaged his hand. 'You should get out now,' I said. 'If you stay, you'll be in great danger.'

'If I leave my hotel, it will be destroyed.'

'Perhaps, but if you stay, they will loot it anyway. Don't let them kill you too. You must leave now.'

He turned away and disappeared into his office. A moment later, I heard the sound of the key being turned.

We went downstairs to the deserted kitchens, took some more water and a little food, and then slipped out of the back door of the hotel and ran off down the access road to the beach.

We sprinted along the sands, using the dunes flanking the beach to screen us from any pursuers. We ran for half a mile, then threw ourselves down, gasping for breath.

'We can't stop yet,' I said, as soon as I could speak. I grabbed a handful of dead palm fronds. 'Come on. Down to the sea.'

When we reached the water's edge, I led Layla through the shallows for another few hundred yards. Then, lungs bursting, I stopped again. I turned to make sure the beach was still empty behind us, then gave Layla the rifle and sent her on ahead into the dunes. I followed, walking backwards, erasing our tracks with the palm fronds.

Layla found a hiding place among the dunes from where we

could keep watch. I swept away the last marks we had made and then lay down beside her. I could feel her heart pounding, but when she turned to speak to me her voice was level. 'What now?'

'We wait for nightfall and then move out.'

CHAPTER 9

We lay there throughout the day, eking out our precious water supply and using the palm fronds to give us a little shelter from the sun. The faraway sounds of shots, screams and explosions continued, but the only visible movement was the flapping of the circling vultures.

Then, in late afternoon, a utility truck crammed with soldiers cruised slowly out of the approach road and down the beach. I sank back deeper into hiding, as they slowed and stopped at the tracks leading down to the sea. Four rebels jumped down and began pacing the beach, staring down towards the sea and back towards the dunes. I inched the rifle forward and eased off the safety catch.

I felt Layla tense as one of the rebels appeared to stare directly at us. 'Keep still,' I said. 'I'm sure they can't see us. Don't move and give us away.' I squeezed her hand and felt an answering pressure.

They began to drive on slowly down the beach. I saw their heads swivel from side to side as they scanned the edge of the dunes. I froze, hardly daring to breathe as they drew level with us. From high in the dunes I could still see faint marks where I had brushed away our tracks. I could only pray they were invisible from beach level.

The truck slowed and then moved on out of sight, but we remained motionless, listening to the engine note. It faded then swelled again, as they turned and began to make their way back.

The truck came into sight, moving even more slowly, and stopped again at the line of tracks. We heard the murmur of voices rising as an argument began, then there was a crash of gears and it drove off again, speeding away up the beach towards the city.

Even when nightfall came we remained where we were, for in the darkness we still heard the occasional burst of firing and the sounds of shouts and brutish laughter, carried to us on the breeze.

Towards midnight Layla said, 'Come on. We can't stay here for ever.'

We moved off through the dunes, slowly working our way along the fringes of the beach. We needed water. My plan was to get some from the hotel if it seemed safe to do so, and then strike across the city to the Medicaid International compound. If we found that untouched, I would leave Layla there and make my way on alone to the High Commission, to obtain some means of communicating with Decisive Measures HQ.

We inched our way along the edge of the approach road from the beach and lay in the shadows behind the hotel for some minutes. There were no lights on and no sign of movement. After watching for ten minutes, I took a last careful look around, then reached across and squeezed Layla's hand. 'OK,' I said. 'Let's go for it.'

We broke cover and sprinted for the back of the hotel, flattening ourselves against the wall at the corner of the building. We edged along it, ducking under the windows, until we reached the rear door. It hung slightly ajar, banging softly in the breeze.

I slid the safety catch off my rifle and eased the door further open with my toe, then paused and listened. There was no sound but the faint drip of water from somewhere inside.

We moved into the dark deserted basement. Everything had been looted. The kitchens were stripped and even the sink and cooker had been ripped from the wall and carried off. All that was left were broken pipes and smashed tiles.

We slaked our thirst and refilled our empty water bottles from a dripping pipe and then crept up the stairs to the ground floor. It was deserted, but everything of value had again been torn out in an orgy of destruction. As we moved through the lobby, our boots crunching on broken glass, I heard a faint noise from the owner's office.

I motioned Layla to silence and crept round the broken brick plinth on which the reception counter had stood. I listened at the door, eased it open a chink and then burst into the room.

A bruised, bloodied figure sat in the far corner, half-burrowed into a pile of broken furniture and fallen plaster. He was rocking slowly to and fro, keening to himself.

It was the hotel owner. He looked up at me for a moment then scrambled to his feet. 'My English friends, thank God, you have come back.'

His speech was slurred, and as his mouth gaped open, I saw by the moonlight the stumps of broken teeth.

'Are there soldiers with you?' His smile faded as I shook my head.

'Are the rebels still here?' I said.

He shuddered and shook his head. 'All gone. Everything gone.'

'Other people?'

Again he shook his head. 'I don't know. I don't know.'

'Do you have food?'

'Nothing. Nothing.'

I left him there. We hurried through the rest of the ground floor searching for food, but the rebels had stripped the place bare. We paused just inside the broken doors of the hotel, peering out into the dark. At last I stepped out again into the heat of the night.

The streets were almost deserted and the handful of people we did see were as nervous and frightened as we were, scuttling away into hiding as soon as they saw us approaching. We kept to the side streets as much as possible and moved a few yards at a time, pausing to scan the way ahead from each doorway or alley.

There was devastation on all sides and mingling with the stink of smoke was the sickly stench of blood. Several times we had to step over corpses, but we saw no other living thing save the rats sharing the fruits of the rebels' victory.

The double doors of the World Food Programme's warehouse stood wide open and the building had been completely emptied of rice. Layla's workplace lay a few yards further down the street. Here again the gates of the compound were unmanned and gaping open. We crept across the yard and entered the darkened building.

We searched it from one end to the other. There were no signs of struggle, no bloodstains, and few bullet holes, but there was no trace of the doctors and nurses who had worked here either and the store rooms had been stripped of every last drug and dressing.

Layla's shoulders sagged. 'What's happened to them?' she said.

I cradled her to my chest. 'They'll be all right,' I said. 'Even if they didn't get away in time, the rebels know the value of them both as medics and as hostages. They'll be well treated.'

She exhaled heavily, still staring around her. 'So what now?'

'The High Commission. Let's hope that hasn't been looted too.'

We had been walking for about twenty minutes when we reached the junction of a broad street and a narrow alley running up the hill in roughly the direction we wanted to follow. We inched our way along the alley, paused at the corner listening and looking, then sprinted across a broad street and dived into another alleyway. As we did so, I heard a shout and the sound of running feet.

We sprinted up the alley. There was another shout followed by the crack of a rifle. I heard the howl and whine of the bullet as it smashed against the wall and ricocheted away.

The words of a combat-survival briefing I had been given as a rookie pilot came into my mind: 'Bullets ride walls. If you're trapped in a street and you have no cover, you're safer in the middle than pressed flat against the walls.'

The theory was fine, the practice less attractive. More shots rang out and more rounds whistled past us. I dived into a doorway, heaving at the door and trying to ignore the running feet and the hail of bullets whining around us. The wood creaked, groaned and at last gave way and we tumbled into a single deserted room.

The running footsteps stopped. There was a moment's silence, then a grenade exploded outside the sagging door. The blast threw us against the wall. I heard a thunderous concussion and a flash of heat seared me. There was the sour taste of chemicals in my mouth.

We dragged ourselves up. The stout door now hung from one hinge, part-blocking the doorway. It had absorbed much of the shrapnel that would otherwise have shredded us. We were both scratched and cut but otherwise unhurt.

Through the ringing in my ears, I heard the sound of running feet again. There was no way out but the way we had come.

I looked up. Thick beams supported the shallow, pitched roof above us. Blackened and ancient, they sagged in the middle and sprouted fungus where they joined the walls. I could only pray that they would bear our additional weight.

The running feet were closer now, almost at the doorway. I threw myself upwards and my fingers grabbed and caught on a beam. I hauled myself onto it, squeezing between the beam and the roof, the muscles of my arms screaming with the effort, then reached down and pulled Layla up and alongside me.

I put my mouth close to her ear. 'Lie on your side along the beam and don't move.' She gave a small nod and did as I said.

We lay lengthways, head to head, our hands clasped. A moment later, the remnants of the door were kicked aside and there was the thunder of automatic weapons.

The shooting stopped. The walls were riddled with bullet holes. There was a pause, then two figures darkened the doorway.

They began firing upwards. Rounds blasted through the roof on either side of us. More rounds smacked into the beam beneath me. I felt it twitch with the impacts and splinters of wood filled the air.

The shooting seemed to go on for ever. I shook with fright, wanting to scream out my terror, beg, plead, anything to make it stop. There was a sudden pause. I heard voices. Then the dark shadows disappeared from the doorway. I fought the urge to peer down.

The next moment there was the thunder of another grenade below us. I heard a rumble as part of the rear wall collapsed. The beam we were lying on twisted and we fell together, crashing down among a torrent of falling masonry and timber. I hit the ground with a thump that drove the breath from my lungs and lay there, helpless, as fragments of stone and tile crashed down around and on top of me.

I heard rough laughter. A few moments later there was the faraway sound of footsteps retreating up the alley.

As the ringing in my ears slowly subsided, I managed to raise my head a little, forced my right arm up through the dead weight of rubble, then clawed at the mound covering me. It took several minutes of gruelling work to prise myself free. My eyes and mouth were gritty with dust and I had suffered cuts and bruises, but I was alive.

I looked around, panicking as I realised that Layla lay buried under the rubble. Then I spotted a foot protruding from the mound. I tore at the rubble until I found the beam, which now lay across her chest.

I dragged and scraped at the stones and dirt covering her head and found myself looking into Layla's eyes. They were red-rimmed and lined with dirt, and her face was covered in blood from a score of cuts. She was shaking with fright.

'Are you badly hurt?' I said.

'I—I don't think so. Just very fr . . . ' Her voice faltered and died.

'Can you move your legs? Your body? Your chest?'

Each time there was hesitation, then the faintest of nods. I felt for the underside of the beam and moved my hand along it. There was a fraction of an inch between her body and the beam, no more.

I glanced around. The building had almost completely collapsed. We were out in the open air, lit by the stars and the setting moon.

I turned back to Layla. 'I can't lift the beam off you, it's too heavy. I'm going to try to pull you out from under it.'

The lower end of the beam was wedged fast against the ground, buried in a mound of stones. The upper end was precariously poised, resting on a mound of loose material. I packed it as well as I could, forcing rocks and broken timbers under it. When I was satisfied that it wouldn't shift, I started to clear the rubble away from one side of Layla's body.

Her frightened face looked up at me. I leaned over and kissed her forehead. 'It's all right, you can do it.'

I pulled gently on her upper arm as she wriggled and strained to free herself. Each movement set off tiny avalanches of dust and stone fragments, causing me to look anxiously at the beam above her. She worked her legs and hips free, but her upper body was still directly under the beam. 'I can't get any further,' she said.

I took hold of her ankles. 'I'm going to try to pull you out.' Her face, beneath the streaks of dirt, looked deathly pale in the faint moonlight. I took hold and began to pull, steadily increasing the pressure on her legs. She moved a little towards me, then stuck. I saw her bite her lip as she tried to stop herself crying out with pain. I let go of her legs. 'It's no good. You're well and truly stuck. I'm going to have to try to lever the beam up a fraction.'

She was silent, but at last I heard her murmur, 'All right.'

I clambered back over the rubble towards what had been the front of the house. One side of the doorway still stood; the rest had collapsed. I leaned out and peered up and down the alley. There was no one in sight and not a sound to be heard.

I took hold of the thick post that had formed one upright of the door frame and began to heave on it, working it to and fro. Dust and mortar dropped away from it and each time I was able to rock it a little further. Finally the fixings gave way. I pulled the timber free, and carried it back to the rubble heap where Layla was buried.

I forced it in under the beam as close to Layla's head as I dared. 'When you feel it lift,' I said, 'scramble for your life . . . Ready?'

I took the strain and then heaved down on one end of the timber, it creaked ominously and for a moment nothing happened. I redoubled my effort. The blood was pounding at my temples and the veins stood out on my arms. There was a creak and a rustle of dust and stone and the beam rose an inch. '*Now, now!*'

Her legs kicked and her head disappeared from my sight under the beam as she wormed her way downwards. The timber creaked once more then split with a crack like a pistol shot. The beam crashed down, the mound of rubble collapsing beneath it. I dropped the useless end of the timber and dragged my eyes towards the other side of the beam. The top of Layla's head was a bare inch from the beam. She rolled over and dragged herself to her feet.

'Thank God,' I said. I crushed her to me and kissed her face, clinging to her, as our tears made tracks in the dust on our cheeks.

She returned my kiss then eased my arms from round her and began gingerly feeling her ribs.

'Anything broken?'

'I don't think so.'

The sky was still dark, but the eastern horizon was tinged with the faintest trace of red. 'We have to move,' I said. 'It'll be day-break soon and if we're caught on the streets . . .'

Hugging the wall, we moved away through the deserted alley.

We paused before each crossroads then hurried on, moving up the hillside using whatever cover we could find.

As we neared the intersection with the main road to the east, we lay flat and crawled our way forward, then paused by the edge of the road, hidden by the rubble from a collapsed shop front. I could hear the crack and whine of small arms and the thunder of heavy weapons from the direction of the airport.

Layla's expression was bleak. I squeezed her arm. 'It gives us some hope. It shows the rebels are still being resisted.' As I spoke, I glimpsed two shapes outlined against the sky over the airport and heard the distant howl of jet engines. 'The rebels don't have any ground-attack planes,' I said. 'The Nigerians might be on the way in.'

Peering through the tangle of broken timbers on top of the mound of rubble, I could see a steady stream of people moving slowly along the road. They were unarmed civilians, and there seemed no sense or purpose in their movement. If they were fleeing from the fighting, they were fleeing in both directions, for as many were heading towards the hills as were trudging towards the centre of the city. Old men, women and children plodded past us. There were no teenage boys or girls or young men or women to be seen, however. I could guess what their fate had been.

As the last of the refugees disappeared from sight, we crossed the road. With the sky lightening by the minute, we had to press on, hoping there would be no rebel patrols or roadblocks.

We worked our way up the hillside, starting at every faint sound. I almost wept with relief when at last I saw the harsh white light over the gates of the High Commission.

We still had a hundred yards of open ground to cross. I took a careful look around us and then we sprinted across the road, the sound of our footfalls seeming to thunder in the semidarkness as we ran.

The High Commission was a concrete blockhouse, protected by steel-barred gates and an eight-foot wall topped with razor wire.

The gates were locked and the door of the guardhouse beyond was closed. I saw a dark figure outlined behind the bulletproof windows and could hear faint music from inside. I called in a low voice. There was no response. I took another look around and then shook the gates. The metallic rattle seemed deafening to me, but still the man did not look up.

I heard the noise of an engine lower down the hillside behind us. I scrabbled frantically in the dirt and at last my fingers closed round a clod of earth. I picked it up and hurled it through the gates at the window. There was a dull thud and the guard stared at us, shaking his head with disapproval. He opened the door, his rifle loose in his right hand. 'What do you want?'

My heart sank. What we needed right now was a trained British soldier, not some local recruit.

'We're British citizens. We need to speak to the High Commissioner.'

He shook his head. 'My orders are to admit no one.'

I heard the noise of the engine growing louder behind us. 'Then get your boss here now,' I said.

'He's asleep.'

'This is life or death. Wake him up.'

'If I do that, I'll be in trouble,' he said.

The noise of the engine grew still louder. There was no time for further discussion. I swung the rifle up to cover him. 'If you don't, you'll be dead. Now drop your rifle and walk towards the gates.'

He put the rifle down and began to move slowly towards the gates, a sheen of sweat on his brow. The glow of headlights lit up the sky behind us and the engine note grew to a roar.

'Faster,' I said. 'Now open the gates.'

He opened his mouth to argue, but I pushed the rifle forward and the barrel dug into his ribs. He stepped to the side of the gates and pushed a button. There was the whine of an electric motor and a rumble as the massive steel gates began to slide slowly apart.

As soon as the gap was wide enough, we squeezed through. 'Now shut them.'

He pressed the button again. As the gates began to close again, the vehicle I had heard cleared the top of the hill behind us.

It skidded to a halt. There were shouts and then a ragged volley of shots as we dived for the cover of the guardhouse. Rounds pinged off the steel gates and one smacked into the bulletproof glass of the window. After another volley of shots I heard the pick-up drive on.

I jabbed the barrel of my rifle into the guard again. 'Now get your superior,' I said.

We followed him into the guardhouse. He picked up the phone and dialled a number, his eyes fixed on the muzzle of my rifle. I heard a distorted voice giving a sleepy reply, and the guard gabbled an explanation. 'I'm being held at the gate by armed gunmen,' he said.

'British armed gunmen,' I shouted.

A moment later a siren began to sound. The seconds ticked by with no sign of movement from the building. Then suddenly the door of the High Commission swung open. As it did so, I saw a flurry of movement to either side of the building, and armed soldiers sprinted out and dived for cover.

I had no wish to be shot by British soldiers so I kept myself clearly visible through the armoured windows of the guardhouse as I held the rifle away from my body and dropped it to the ground. Then I raised my hands over my head and Layla did the same.

A voice barked at us from the darkness. 'Step forward, five paces. Now down! Down!'

I spread-eagled myself in the dirt and heard Layla drop alongside me. There was the sound of running feet, and my arms were grabbed and jerked up behind my back. I winced as the flexicuffs bit into my wrists. Then I was hauled to my feet.

'Who are you?'

'Jack Griffiths. Helicopter pilot with Decisive Measures.'

'Who's she?'

Layla replied for herself. 'Layla Edwards, a paramedic with Medicaid International.'

'We were shot down upcountry a few days ago,' I said. 'We made it back to Freetown just in time to be caught up in the coup.'

'It's not been your lucky week, has it? Where's your ID?' Already the voice was friendlier.

I jerked my head towards my pocket. One of the soldiers took our documents and passed them to his boss. He checked them.

'OK,' he said. 'Bring them inside.' We were hustled in through the main door of the building. 'And you can lose the cuffs,' he said. As they were removed, I rubbed the feeling back into my wrists.

We were shown into a room. A moment later an attaché strode in. I took his outstretched hand. 'Glad you made it,' he said. 'We were worried about you.'

I outlined our experiences. When I fell silent, he wrinkled his nose. 'Now, from the state of you, I'd say you need a shower, fresh clothes, something to eat and a stiff drink. Get yourselves cleaned up and then I'll have someone show you to the dining room. You'll find someone else there who will be even more pleased to see you.' He had walked out before I could ask him who he was talking about.

I spent a long time in the shower, soaping the filth and sweat from my body. I was covered in cuts, bruises and mosquito bites, some already turning septic, but it could have been a lot worse. When I was ready I dressed in clean clothes—not my own, but approximately the right size—and followed a soldier to the dining room.

As I entered, Grizz leapt up from a table and clasped me in a bear hug, nearly crushing my ribs. 'I didn't expect to see you again,' he said. 'You're either a military genius or the luckiest bastard alive.'

'You must be a bit of a lucky sod yourself,' I said.

He shrugged. 'Those rebels are brave but they're not soldiers. I just kept firing and moving. Their leader called them off in the end. I probably had the same idea as you—head for Freetown, not Bohara. Luckily, when I hit the road I was able to'—he paused and smiled—'to borrow a pick-up from a group of rebels I came across. They didn't look like they had any further use for it by then. I was parked up here waiting for orders from HQ when the coup started.'

He broke off as Layla came in, and hugged her. 'Great to see you,' he said. 'Now, you two eat and I'll talk. Here's the situation.' He gave a grim smile. 'As you've probably already noticed, the city's disintegrated—no police, no army, no one in control. The Nigerians are holding the airport and have apparently started a push out towards the city, but I'm not too optimistic about their enthusiasm for a fight if the rebels make a stand.'

'Do you think they will?'

'Hard to know. Their usual practice is to loot everything they can carry and then take off for the hills. The Nigerians won't pursue them there. The rebels might let them have Freetown for now; what they really want are the diamond mines.

'Anyway, we've been given three objectives: to help secure the existing government in power if possible, to evacuate European workers if necessary—but only if necessary—and to hold the diamond mines at all costs.' He gave a sour smile. 'Not necessarily in that order. Our first job is to get as much ammunition as we can carry up to Bohara. The garrison's still holding off the attacks at the moment, but once the rebels have finished looting the capital, the odds are they'll begin an all-out assault on the mines. We need to be there to help fight them off, or get our guys out before they're wiped out.'

I glanced towards Layla. 'What about the Medicaid people?'

Grizz shrugged. 'No sign of them and no ransom demands yet.'

Layla said nothing, but I saw her expression as she turned away.

'Try not to worry,' I said to her. 'Like I told you, they won't be harmed. They're too valuable to the rebels.'

'Anyway,' Grizz said, 'the boys at Bohara are in shit street. They're low on supplies and ammunition and hard-pressed by the rebels. Now we've got you back, though, we're in with a shout, apart from one big problem. Her Majesty's Government are running scared about being seen to support our activities. Which means that despite our friendly welcome here, the supply of helis or heavy weapons is not going to be permitted. They won't even look the other way this time while we bring them in from elsewhere.'

'So what can we do?' I said. 'The heli's in pieces in the jungle.'

He shook his head. 'There is one more.'

I stared at him for a moment, then I shook my head. 'Oh no. You're not thinking of that wreck at Camp Seventeen, are you?'

He nodded. 'Exactly.'

'We'd never get it off the ground.'

'We'll have a bloody good try. What else can we do? The rebels are pounding Bohara. We need to give our guys some fire support.'

I looked around. Layla was sitting at the other end of the table, sipping a cup of coffee as if it were the most beautiful thing she had ever tasted. I lowered my voice. 'What about Layla?' I said.

'She comes with us, of course. There are wounded at Bohara.'

'No!' I almost shouted it.

'You were happy enough to have her along before,' Grizz said.

'That was different.'

'I think I'm entitled to a voice in this,' Layla said. She had walked the length of the table and now stood directly behind me. 'I'm going back to Bohara with you.'

'It's too risky, Layla, too dangerous,' I said.

She smiled. 'More dangerous than what we've been through already?'

'But we had to do that; you don't have to do this.'

'I'm a medic, Jack. Of course I have to.'

'But you can't—' I began.

Her eyes flashed. 'Don't presume to tell me what I can and can't do. I'm doing my work, just as you're doing yours. I'm going to Bohara with you. End of story.'

I was ready to go on with the argument, but her expression showed me I'd be wasting my time.

'Anyway,' I said, turning back to Grizz, 'how do we get to Camp Seventeen without a vehicle?'

'We've got the one I borrowed.'

'And what do we do for weapons?'

He winked and tapped his nose. 'The High Commissioner is not unsympathetic. Officially he can't do anything, of course, but unofficially . . . he's been looking the other way while I've called in a couple of favours from the garrison here.'

'But what about spare parts for the heli?'

'What we have, we'll use. What we don't, we'll improvise.'

'So when do we leave?'

'As soon as we're ready,' he said. 'I'll just get the latest situation report here and call HQ for an update, then we're on our way.'

He returned to the room a few minutes later. 'The Nigerians' push out along the airport road ended after a couple of miles,' he said. 'They pulled back at the first sign of resistance. No surprises there. HQ reckons they'll just hold the airport and await developments.'

He led the way to the compound at the back of the High Commission. A battered utility truck was parked there. Two general-purpose machine guns had been lashed onto it, on either side of the roll bar. 'OK,' he said. 'Layla will drive. You and I'll take charge of the guns. Have you fired one before?'

I shook my head.

'With luck, the threat should be enough anyway. But if we meet any roadblocks and the usual cigarettes and bribes don't do the trick, use very short bursts. It'll save ammunition and it'll stop you from shooting up the treetops instead of the rebels.'

I helped him to load fuel, water and rations, and we shoved a few cartons of cigarettes under the dashboard. Then we climbed in the back and Layla gunned the engine.

CHAPTER 10

We bucketed out of the gate in a cloud of dust and I hung on to the roll bar for support as we bounced down the road. It was early in the morning and most of the rebel soldiers were no doubt sleeping off the previous night's looting and drinking.

We tore through the outskirts of the city with Layla at the wheel, swerving expertly around piles of rubble, abandoned vehicles and the remains of barricades. As we turned onto the road towards the mountains, however, we hit a roadblock guarded by eight soldiers.

Grizz swung the barrel of his GPMG to cover them. I followed suit, keeping a particularly wary eye on a man with an RPG. 'Government soldiers or rebels?' I asked.

'Who knows?' Grizz said. 'They look more like government men, but it doesn't necessarily make any difference anyway.' With the forefinger of his right hand curled round the trigger of his weapon, he raised the other hand, palm outwards in a gesture of friendship.

Layla pulled out a carton of cigarettes and held it out of the window. One of the soldiers took it from her. They shared the cigarettes out, but still made no move to raise the barrier.

'Where are you going to?' their leader said.

'Just to the hills to try to buy food.'

'Not to Bohara?'

'See for yourself, we have nothing here, just water and a little fuel.'

The soldiers debated among themselves, staring at the GPMGs. Finally the leader shrugged. 'Twenty dollars and you can pass.'

'We have only leones,' Grizz lied.

The leader motioned one of his soldiers forward and Grizz handed him a bundle of crumpled notes. The leader counted them, then jerked his head to his men, who began dismantling the barricade.

We ground on up the hill, turned off the main road and followed the winding track through the forest. We were on maximum alert as we approached the base, but the familiar listless soldiers still sprawled in the dust by the fire-blackened buildings inside the fence. They jumped to their feet and shouldered their weapons when they heard our approach, but at the sight of Grizz and yet another carton of cigarettes they dragged the gates open.

We drove into the compound and across to the rusting helicopter. Layla and I stripped the dust-laden camouflage net from it as Grizz disappeared into the Nissen hut and began dragging out spare parts, tools and a pile of what looked like scrap metal.

I looked the heli over and shook my head. 'We'll never fix this.'

Grizz brandished a roll of metallic tape. 'There's nothing that can't be fixed with speed tape.'

I began checking the heli externally, while Grizz worked on the engine. Then I began bolting lengths of aluminium section across the worst of the holes in the cab walls.

It was four hours before Grizz was satisfied with the engines. We paused for a brew and a bite to eat, then I ran through the cockpit checks while Grizz removed the GPMGs from the pick-up, fixed brackets improvised from scrap metal to the door frame of the heli and bound the guns to them with swaths of speed tape.

Next he beckoned to me and I followed him into the Nissen hut. Together we dragged a rocket pod from the hut and levered it into position on the underside of the nose of the cockpit. I tried to blank off the memory of what had happened the last time I had fired a rocket pod in action, but the thought kept returning to me.

When it was securely attached, Grizz connected a firing cable to the trigger on the stem of the collective, holding it in place with speed tape.

I helped Grizz to load the rocket pods and we took on maximum fuel and maximum ammunition for the mini-guns. When we had finished, the helicopter looked as if it had been assembled from scrap metal and Meccano, and bound together with speed tape.

I did the preflight checks and then pressed the starter. The turbine stuttered and whined like an old banger on a frosty morning. Then the engine coughed and died as a cloud of black smoke belched out. I exchanged a glance with Grizz, then tried again. Once more it faltered, spluttered and then caught. I tried the other engine and the whine of the turbines swelled to a roar as it also caught and fired. Grizz gave a thumbs-up and ran for the cab. The heli seemed in surprisingly good mechanical nick. I let the engines idle for five minutes as I checked the gauges, watching for any warning signs.

I glanced across at Layla in the copilot's seat. Her expression was relaxed, but the whiteness of her knuckles and the way she caught her lip between her teeth showed how nervous she was.

I reached across to squeeze her arm with my gloved hand, then I pushed the lever into flight idle. I raised the collective and eased the cyclic forward as we rose from the ground, and I paddled the rudder pedals, banking us to the east.

The Huey's response to the controls was sluggish, but that was hardly surprising. Even through my helmet I was deafened by the noise as the slipstream howled through the bullet holes in the body, setting metal vibrating against metal in a cacophony of noise.

There was only sporadic ground fire as we flew over the outskirts of the capital. Looking down, I could see smoke still rising from scores of fires. Ragged lines of vehicles were moving in both directions, empty trucks and pick-ups heading into the city, and heavily laden ones making for the mountains to the east.

The airport road was scarred with the marks of recent fighting, the road surface blackened, burned and part-blocked by the wrecks of vehicles. Bodies still lay sprawled in the dirt around them.

The two Hawk jets I had seen flying sorties the previous night were drawn up on the hard standing at the far side of the airfield, near a couple of Nigerian military transport planes that were unloading supplies. Groups of soldiers were dug in around the perimeter and a large force of men was milling about near the arrivals hall.

I kept the heli high until the last possible moment, then made a steep descent over the heart of the airfield to touch down safely.

We climbed down from the Huey and followed Grizz over to the main airport building. A group of Nigerian officers had commandeered the airport administration offices for their own use.

Grizz introduced himself to the senior officer, a bulky figure in combat fatigues and the inevitable mirrored sunglasses.

'What's the situation here, Major?' Grizz asked.

'We have secured the airfield,' he said. 'When we are ready, we shall advance on Freetown and drive the rebels back into the hills.'

We walked over to the small barbed-wire compound that Decisive Measures maintained at the airport. Some of the Sierra Leonean soldiers detailed to guard it were still there, but they seemed cowed by the presence of the Nigerians.

There was no sign that there had been any fighting in the immediate area, but there had been a serious attempt to force the locks on the heavy steel doors of the store bunkers. In one case it had been successful. The doors hung off their hinges and the interior of the bunker had been stripped bare.

'The rebels?' I said.

Grizz shook his head. 'They never breached the airport perimeter. More likely our saviours here.'

He walked over and spoke to the Nigerians. All shook their heads or shrugged their shoulders.

Grizz led the Sierra Leonean soldiers off to one side and began talking to them. I couldn't hear what they said, but their body language showed their uneasiness. They kept their faces averted from Grizz's probing stare and raised their eyes only to dart nervous glances at the Nigerians.

Grizz pointed a finger towards the city. 'You want to keep working for us? Or do you want to take your chances out there?'

A couple of the men hesitated, then muttered something in reply. He walked back to us. 'Come on.'

We made our way back to the administration building. The Nigerian officer made no attempt to conceal his impatience as Grizz stated his grievance. 'One of our store bunkers has been looted of grenades, rifles and ammunition.'

'Of what concern is this to me?'

'Your men are the culprits.'

'You dare to accuse my men of this? Where is your proof?'

'The word of the soldiers we pay to guard it.' He paused. 'If we don't get them back, those weapons will be sold to the rebels who have been robbing, raping and killing in Freetown, while your men sit here doing nothing. Are you here to protect the people or are you waiting for the rebels to leave so that you and your men can take their turn at whatever is left?'

The Nigerian strode from behind his desk and stood toe to toe with Grizz. 'We are Africans.' He jabbed his stubby thumb into his chest. 'I am African. These are my people, they have my protection. We Africans know who the real oppressors are. Get out before I have you arrested.'

'Go ahead. See how much shit hits the fan after that. With the amount we pay in bribes to Nigerian generals, I don't think we'll have any difficulty in finding one willing to bust you back down to private.' He paused. 'We want those weapons back, Major, and if any of those other bunkers are tampered with again, we'll be asking our generals for a favour.'

'Do Decisive Measures really have some Nigerian generals on the payroll?' I asked as we walked back across the airfield.

Grizz laughed. 'I don't know, but you'd have to be a brave major to call the bluff, wouldn't you?' He opened one of the other bunkers and we loaded more ammunition for the garrison at Bohara. Then I fired up the engines and took off, staying above the safe haven of the airport as I maintained a tight spiral climb to height.

I levelled at 2,000 feet and set the nose of the Huey directly towards Bohara. The landscape had been transformed into a scene of devastation. Villages had become blackened ruins, their fields stripped bare of crops. Everywhere there were fleeing figures, scattering in panic at the sight of the helicopter. Whether they were rebels, government troops or simply refugees it was impossible to know.

We dropped into the Bohara Valley. Grizz and I began a three-way conversation with the radio operator at the mine compound. Grizz was also talking to Rudi on the net.

'We need to get the expats out,' the operator said. 'The mines have been shut down for the last week anyway and we're taking a storm of incoming fire. We can't guarantee their safety any longer.'

'Have them ready to ship out,' I said.

Grizz chipped in. 'Hostiles are reported advancing twelve miles. Let's see if we can quieten those bastards down first before we start worrying about the expats.'

We passed over the compound and swung away onto the bearing Grizz indicated. We swooped over a ridge line and down towards the target valley. As if my Kosovo nightmare had again become reality, I saw a burning hamlet ahead of me, the ruined buildings standing stark among the flames and smoke. Beyond it was dense woodland and forest.

As I skimmed along the tree line, the downwash lashing at the branches revealed shapes moving in the shadows of the trees. There were no muzzle flashes, no tick of rounds against the Huey's skin. I could see figures running between the trees but I had no way of telling if they were refugees from the burning village or rebel soldiers.

Not again, please God, not again, I thought. I made another, slower pass. Still there was no fire from the woods.

I flicked the intercom switch. 'What do you get, Grizz?'

'Figures. Hostiles.'

'They could be villagers.'

'Negative. I can see men with weapons.'

'They might be sticks or spears,' I said. 'Hold your fire, I'll make another pass.' I did, and then another, putting the heli into a hover directly in front of the half-hidden figures, inviting them to shoot.

I heard the clank of the ammunition links for the door gun.

'Hold your fire.'

'What?' Grizz said. 'Jesus, Jack. What are you trying to do?'

I ignored him, my thoughts echoing in my brain: *Why don't they shoot? Why don't they shoot?*

I glanced at Layla. Her face showed her fear, but her voice was firm and level. 'This isn't Kosovo, Jack,' she said. 'Trust your judgment. Do what you have to do.'

I strained to look beyond the camouflage of the foliage. I saw a few angular shapes and what might have been the glint of metal. Then the sunlight glancing from the metal fuselage of the heli was picked up and reflected by a score of tiny mirrors, gleaming like Christmas lights in the darkness of the forest.

That decided me. I had seen enough rebels with mirror fragments woven into their hair or dangling from their clothing, part of the juju they believed would ward off evil and keep them alive.

I swung the heli away from the forest then banked in a sweeping turn. 'Are you ready in the back?' I said.

The answer from Grizz was immediate. 'Just give me the word.'

'On my shot.' My finger began to close on the trigger. A microsecond before I fired, a figure came sprinting from the tree line—a woman blundering directly into the cross hairs of my sights.

The vision of the burning woman from Kosovo flooded my mind. 'Abort! Abort! Abort!' I pulled my hand from the trigger as if it had been burned, and banked us up and left, away from the wood.

'Jack? What's going on? Jack?'

I couldn't answer him for a moment. My hands were trembling so much I could barely grip the controls and my body shook with shivers. I offered a silent prayer of thanks that I'd been saved from repeating the terrible crime I'd committed in Kosovo.

I glanced back over my shoulder and saw the woman still running. Then she stopped, jerking from side to side as if some giant invisible hand was shaking her. She toppled forward and lay still.

Then there was a red flash from the edge of the wood and I heard Grizz's warning shout. 'Missile launch! Evade! Evade! Evade!' I was already throwing the Huey into a savage right-hand break as the RPG round blasted up at me trailing a plume of dirty grey smoke. I watched it with a curious detachment as it knifed past us, so close it appeared to pass through the whirling disc of the rotors. Then it was gone, diminishing to a black speck in the sky, before it exploded in a ball of orange flame.

I glanced down. At once I glimpsed the stooping figure of a rebel soldier, a squat black tube extending from his shoulder. I swung the heli back to face the forest.

The rebel soldier had reloaded and was raising the launcher back to his shoulder. He froze as he saw the Huey blasting in towards him. I nudged the nose of the heli right a shade, and as the cross hairs intersected, I squeezed the firing trigger. There was a *whoosh* as the rocket blasted from the pod. The soldier disappeared in a burst of crimson flame and clods of earth were blasted into the air.

I heard the clatter of the GPMG as Grizz began raking the tree line. He gave a warning shout. 'Muzzle flashes four o'clock.' I swung the heli right to bring my weapons to bear and squeezed the trigger of the rocket pod again. Driven by a cold rage, I attacked over and over, indifferent to danger, as I laid the ghosts of my past. I was wreaking vengeance as much for what I had done in Kosovo as for the terror the rebels had inflicted here.

I launched all the rockets from the pod and kept firing the nose gun long after every sign of movement from the rebels had ceased, then I turned away, back towards Bohara.

Suddenly there was a flash and a blast strong enough to throw the Huey sideways. Shrapnel ripped into the side of the cab.

'What the—' I froze. In the corner of my eye I glimpsed a black shape just above the forest canopy, as sinister and ugly as a tarantula, but far more deadly.

It was a Hind helicopter gunship. The markings on its flanks had been painted out, but there was little doubt where it had come from. The Liberians had obviously decided to gamble on an intervention to tip the fight for the diamond mines in favour of their protégés.

There was another flash and a streak of smoke and flame. 'Flares! Flares! Flares!' I yelled.

Layla's hand hovered over the buttons, then pressed one.

'Not chaff, flares! The next button!'

She pressed the correct button and the fierce light of miniature stars burned at the periphery of my vision as a burst of flares ignited in our slip-stream.

I put us into a dive even as I spun the heli round to mask the heat of the engines from the missile streaking towards us.

The Huey screamed downwards. I held the dive until my vision was filled with the sight of onrushing trees, then almost broke the Huey's back as I pulled the steepest climbing turn I could manage. I could feel the blood draining from my brain as the G force bit, but I held the turn until the colour began to wash from my vision. It was the grey-out—the prelude to unconsciousness.

I eased back on the controls and, as my full vision returned, I whipped my head round searching for the Hind. 'Where is it?'

'In your five,' Grizz said, hanging out of the door of the cab to keep the enemy in sight. 'Go left. Go left.'

I stamped down on the rudder again, forcing the Huey into another juddering turn. The Hind flashed across my sights. I'd have given a year's wages for just one of the rockets I'd blasted into the forest only a few minutes before, but the pod was empty.

As the cross hairs intersected on the Hind I squeezed the trigger of the nose guns and rounds spat out, punching a rising line though the Hind's fuselage. Then the firing stopped abruptly. I squeezed the trigger again, holding the turn to keep the enemy heli in my sights, but the guns were useless—empty or jammed.

I could barely control a mounting wave of panic. I had no rockets and now no guns—no armaments of any sort to take into a duel with one of the deadliest gunships ever built. And the Hind was already turning to bring its own weapons to bear once more.

I tried to manoeuvre to bring Grizz's guns to bear, but though he loosed off a couple of bursts, sighting through the doorway of the cab barely gave him enough time before the Hind was out of his line of sight again.

The Hind flashed towards me. I faked a left turn, then kicked hard right and dived, passing under the Hind, its blind spot. We were so close that its downwash shook the Huey like a terrier on a rat and my own rotors scythed the air within feet of its metal belly.

In that instant, I saw one glimmer of hope. I accelerated and set the nose due west as if bugging out from the fight and running for home. The Hind immediately turned in pursuit and the gap that had begun to open narrowed again. He was now in perfect position to plant a heat-seeking missile straight into the exhaust of the Huey's straining engines . . .

I dumped the collective and booted the right rudder, sending the Huey into the most savage break yet. There was a strangled cry from Layla alongside me as the force of the turn threw her against the side of the cockpit and I heard a thud and a curse behind me as Grizz lost his footing and fell against the wall of the cab.

The Huey's momentum carried it through the turn and as the nose dipped and we started to drop, a flash of fire trailing smoke blasted past the cockpit mere feet from my face.

It detonated with a blinding flash behind us, but I had no time to spare it a thought. We were now nose to nose, a mile apart and closing fast. If neither of us evaded, we would impact in seconds.

The Hind opened up again with a burst from its nose gun and then jinked left. I matched the move exactly. We were still nose to nose. He went right and left again, then climbed, and each time I matched him, focusing only on the helmeted figure I could just glimpse through the tinted Perspex bubble of the Hind's canopy. We were now no more than 200 yards apart. I sensed as much as saw him start to climb and once more matched his move.

'Jack! What are you doing?' Layla screamed. 'You'll kill us all!'

A fraction of a second later I saw the Hind's nose dip. I twitched the cyclic upwards as its ugly black shape filled my vision. The disturbed air threw the Huey around, but I held the controls with rigid arms as I saw the nose of the Hind slide towards us. I could see the pilot's expression freeze as I jerked the cyclic forward and the Huey began to drop towards the blur of razor-edged motion—the rotors of the Hind.

There was no margin for error. A couple of feet too low or too high, a fraction of a second early or late, and we would all die together. I started to panic. I had left it too late, I had missed.

My hands twitched instinctively on the controls even though I knew the Hind would be long gone before any correction I made now could take effect. Then there was the crack and whine of metal on metal from behind and below me. The back of our skids had caught the tips of the Hind's main rotors.

I was powerless to do anything but wait. If I had misjudged our angle of dive, I would have set us on an irreversible path to destruction. Our own tail rotor would be destroyed, cut to pieces by the massive blades of the Hind's main rotors.

There was a deafening crash and my helmet smacked against the edge of the canopy as the Huey was thrown sideways. The floor of the cockpit beneath my feet was buckled by the impact.

I heard Grizz curse and yell as he was thrown around. The force of the impact had spun us round so that the Hind again filled my vision. Its main rotors were still turning at blinding speed, but the tail had disappeared, smashed away like rotten wood. With no tail rotor to control the torque, the giant body of the Hind was already beginning to spin out of control. Whipping around its own axis, it drilled downwards towards the ground and then disappeared in a massive orange and yellow flash.

I pushed up my visor to wipe the sweat from my eyes. 'Jesus,' I said. 'That's the first and last dogfight I ever want to go into with no ammunition. If they've got another Hind, we're finished.' I heard Grizz's rumbling laugh over the intercom. 'I think you just wrecked at least fifty per cent of the Liberian air force. I don't think there's much danger of them risking the other half as well.'

Layla, too, joined in the laughter, but her face was deathly pale.

CHAPTER 11

I set the heli climbing to clear the ridge, sighting on a notch in the skyline where a landslip had cut away a section like a small quarry. Beneath it the slopes were barren and strewn with scree. 'A great place to hide,' I said as we flashed over it. 'You could lie up there for weeks and never be found.'

We cleared the ridge and flashed down towards Bohara. The ground fire from the rebels began at once and rounds clipped the rotor blades, tracing a brief fiery trail of sparks in the sky.

I pressed down lower and kept the heli weaving from side to side as I radioed the compound, 'Grizzly One, coming in.'

Almost at once the garrison put out a barrage of fire at the rebels. As I dropped fast and low towards the helipad, I could make out people gathered in knots around the perimeter wire, and a jostling mass pressing against the gates of the inner compound. The rebels had driven villagers and mineworkers alike towards Bohara. They were pinned between the advancing rebels and the mercenary garrison. I could see them shouting, pleading and waving fistfuls of leone bills. It felt like the fall of Saigon.

We landed. As the engines wound down, I looked at Layla. 'Your patients are waiting,' I said. 'You haven't got long, though.'

As I spoke, I cast an uneasy glance out of the cockpit. The arrival of the helicopter seemed to have driven the people into a frenzy. They were clawing at the razor wire, indifferent to the cuts on their hands as they tried to haul themselves up and over.

One boy succeeded. He sprawled in the dust and then pulled himself to his feet only to be clubbed to the ground again by a mercenary. I recognised Rudi's powerful figure standing over the prone figure. As the boy raised his face from the dust, Layla stared through the cockpit, then began tearing at her harness.

She jumped down from the cockpit and sprinted towards the fence, ignoring the crackle of small-arms fire. I hurried after her. She was crouching over the boy. I helped her carry him towards the two-storey container building at the centre of the compound.

We laid him down at the side of the doorway and, screened by the wall of sandbags, Layla first tested his skull for fractures and then began to bandage his torn hands. Only when he opened his eyes and spoke did I realise that the boy was Kaba.

Layla was trying to calm him, but he kept gabbling out the same refrain, 'You must come to Boroyende. Njama is wounded.'

'What happened?' I said.

He turned his bleak gaze on me. 'The rebels came. They knew you had been to the village; they'd seen your truck. They said we were spying for you.' He stared me out. 'They found the knife you gave him. They said it was payment for spying. They tried to kill everyone. A few of us managed to get away and hide.'

A sick feeling grew in my stomach. 'But Njama? He is alive?'

He nodded. 'He was in the fields, otherwise they would have killed him too. But he is sick, wounded. He needs medicine.' He turned back to Layla. 'He needs you. You must come.'

Layla took my arm and led me off to one side. 'We have to go there,' she said. 'What's happened is our fault, our responsibility.'

'I can't,' I said. 'I have to take the expat workers out of here.'

'And then?'

'Whatever my orders are next.'

'And the black mineworkers?'

'You know the answer to that, I'm afraid. They're on their own.'

'In other words, you're going to leave them to die.'

I couldn't hold her gaze.

'And Boroyende?'

Again, I couldn't meet her eyes as I answered. 'The same.'

'So, you look after the expats and the diamonds and leave the people themselves to die.'

'It's not that black and white.'

'You're wrong, Jack. Black and white is exactly what it is.'

She stared at me for a moment. There was a look in her eyes I could not read.

'What is it?' I said.

She looked away. 'Nothing,' she said. 'I made a mistake, that's all.'

She turned her back on me before I could reply.

Grizz had been conferring with Rudi and now came racing back to the Huey. 'Let's get things moving, fast.'

A group of white expatriates, each clutching a single case, stood waiting for the signal to load. Fear and anger vied for control of their faces as they stared at the mob outside the compound, held back only by the threat of the mercenaries' guns.

I walked over to Layla, who was huddled in a corner talking to the boy. I touched her shoulder but almost flinched at the look she gave me. 'We have to get ready,' I said.

She shook her head. 'You mean you do. I'm staying here.'

'You can't do that. It's crazy.'

She gave me a level stare. 'You're coming back for the mercenaries, aren't you? Or are they to be left to die too?'

'Of course I'm coming back.'

She shrugged. 'Then I'll return with them.'

Grizz came charging over. 'Jack, for God's sake get out there before that heli's overrun.' I hesitated, still holding Layla's gaze, then I turned and ran for the Huey.

The expatriates ran for it too as I fired up the engines. A crowd of black workers began trying to force the gates of the compound. The massive figures of Hendrik and Reuben were at the heart of a group of mercenaries firing over their heads and into the dust at their feet, trying to hold them back. At a command from Rudi, Reuben turned and jogged to the helicopter. He swung himself up into the cab.

'Grizz? What's going on?' I said into the intercom. 'The Huey's already seriously overloaded. You're the door gunner. We don't need him as well.'

'I'm also the boss,' Grizz said. 'We've two GPMGs. I can't fire both of them and we need every gun hand we can load onto this crate.'

'If we're too overloaded, we won't get airborne.'

'Just try it, will you?'

I hesitated, sick at heart, staring back towards the entrance to the container building, where Layla's slim figure was still hunched in the shadows next to the boy.

'What are you waiting for? Let's get out of here,' Grizz said.

The turbine whined its way up the octaves. I raised the collective to bring the Huey to a hover, but it barely lifted on its springs. I pushed the collective right up to the stops but the heli remained rooted to the ground, shuddering with the vibrations of the engines as they strained at maximum power.

'I'll have to try a running takeoff,' I said.

I used the cyclic to set the heli lumbering slowly across the compound. It ground its way slowly forward, the skid plates scraping and rattling at the earth. If I could squeeze enough momentum out of it to lift the rotors into clean, undisturbed air, free of the turbulence of the ground effect, in theory we would achieve translational lift—the rotors would bite and send us soaring upwards.

That was the aim. At the moment, we were still bumping along the ground, carving furrows in the red dirt of the compound with the skids. Just short of the perimeter fence I paddled the right rudder—turning with the torque increased the available power to the main rotors—and came around.

We accelerated again across the compound. The heli rocked as the skids rumbled over the rutted ground.

We were moving too fast to make another ground turn and the fence was now looming. I hauled on the collective. For a moment the heli remained earthbound, but then I felt a sudden jerk as the rotors bit into clean air, free of the turbulence of the downwash.

As the perimeter wire seemed to rush towards us, we crept a few feet above the earth. I swung the heli around just in time to miss the fence and nosed it back across the compound, barely airborne and still trapped by the fence surrounding us.

We crawled back across the compound, not gaining an inch of altitude. I brought the Huey to a hover a few feet above the floor of the compound. The vibrations increased and after a moment the by now familiar screech of the low RPM warning began to sound.

The battle between power and weight was being lost, and inch by inch the Huey was slowly sinking back towards the ground. I had to find a way to reduce the power demand for a moment or I'd lose control of the ship altogether.

I eased the collective down a fraction, letting the Huey drift downwards. My reward was to hear the turbines pick up. The warning siren died away, and as soon as the heli stabilised I eased the collective up again and the Huey rose back into the air.

Once more, however, even though I pulled in maximum power, as soon as the Huey began to rise out of the ground effect, it started to settle back down again. I repeated the manoeuvre and, perhaps helped by the loss of fuel weight as I kept the engines bellowing, this time I managed to squeeze a few more revs and at last got the Huey level with the top of the compound fence. I kept parallel to it, building the revs as much as I could. Then I took a deep breath and banked hard right, praying that the power boost I could nick from allowing the Huey to swing with the torque would be enough to lift us clear of the fence.

The coils of razor wire along the top disappeared beneath us. I was just beginning to exhale when there was a savage jerk. The nose dipped and I fought the controls to stabilise the heli, holding it in a hover as the engines screamed under the load.

Grizz's voice came over the intercom. 'We're caught. One of the wheels has snagged the razor wire.'

I glanced behind into the cab. He was hanging out of the door. 'I'll have to free it. Get me roped up.'

He wriggled back in and Reuben tied a rope around his chest, padding it with his shirt. Grizz picked up a pair of metal shears from the toolkit and Reuben lowered him out of the door. He hung suspended for a moment out of reach of the wire and the skids. Then Reuben began to swing him like a pendulum.

Slowly at first, Grizz swung away in a wider and wider arc. I heard him grunt as he grabbed and missed the shaft of the skids, then he grabbed again and held.

His voice came again over the intercom. 'Back five.'

I eased the heli back. I saw a strand of wire curl up into my vision as he cut through it and heard his laboured breathing.

A gust of wind hit the heli, pushing it a few feet. 'Hold it,' I said into the intercom, working the controls to bring us back. Just then I heard the snap of the razor wire parting, followed by a scream. The heli lurched and one end of the severed wire lashed the side of the cockpit like a whip. It left a bloody trail across the Perspex.

Reuben's voice cut in on the intercom. 'We've got to land again. Grizz is down there.'

I swung the heli around, craning my neck to look down. A figure lay sprawled in the dirt, one leg twisted underneath him. The flying razor wire had sliced through the rope and sent Grizz plunging to the earth, but the fall was not what had killed him.

The wire had also cut clean through his neck, severing his head.

Reuben's voice came again. 'We have to land.'

'We can't,' I said. 'We're overloaded already and the fence is down. If we land there those guys will rush us. Besides, there's nothing we can do for Grizz. He's dead. We'll have to leave him here.'

'You don't leave a comrade behind, even if he is dead.'

'This time we'll have to. I thought the world of Grizz too, but if we land to pick up his body, we'll never get airborne.' I raised the collective again and pushed the cyclic forward, ending the argument.

The ship groaned and shook as it climbed slowly away from the compound. I flew in a daze, only dimly aware of the landscape passing below me and the feel of the controls in my hands.

At last, in the distance ahead, I saw the surf haze hanging over the coast. Then the grey rutted concrete of the airport runway came into view. As we made our approach, a few bursts of ground fire greeted us, but it was sporadic and barely threatening.

I eased down the collective, flared and landed.

I killed the engines and slumped in my seat, feeling the sweat soaking through my flying suit. The expats tumbled from the heli, laughing and joking as they hurried across the concrete towards the terminal. I went the other way, to the edge of the airfield where I bought some food and a drink from a stall.

I sat down in the shade of a fuel bunker as a fuel bowser trundled across the hard standing towards the Huey. Then I heard the scrunch of feet on the dusty concrete and a shadow fell across me. I looked up.

'Don't get up,' said a clipped, English voice. 'Henry Pleydell. We met at Bohara when you first came out here.'

I nodded. 'I remember you, Colonel.'

'You've done a great job for us, Jack,' he said. 'Grizz has told us.'

'Grizz is dead.'

He pursed his lips, and a bead of sweat trickled down his forehead and splashed onto the front of his neatly pressed shirt. 'I'm very sorry to hear that,' he said. He nodded to himself, then went on, his manner once more brisk and businesslike. 'We have reports that Liberian troops are massing on the frontier. Some may even have crossed it. The mining company is no longer prepared to meet the cost of countering a full-blown invasion. So we're pulling out, Jack, and leaving the Nigerians to fight it out.'

'Until the next time,' I said.

'Oh, I'm sure we'll be back when the situation permits. But in the meantime we need you to fly just a couple more missions, to bring out the rest of the garrison and a package.'

'What sort of package?'

He rolled his eyes. 'It *is* a diamond mine, old boy.' He paused. 'Get airborne as soon as you can. There'll be a healthy bonus in it for you when they're safely delivered.'

'The diamonds or the men?'

A fleeting look of irritation passed across his face. 'Both, of course. You don't think we'd leave them to die, do you?'

'I need a door gunner and a copilot,' I said.

'Door gunner is no problem. Take Reuben. But I'm afraid you'll have to keep flying solo. We've moved heaven and earth to try to find one in these last few days. We even offered double rates, but there were still no takers. People believe all sorts of rumours.'

'Quite,' I said. 'So what ordnance have you got here? Are there rockets for the pod?'

He shook his head. 'Just rounds for the guns, I'm afraid.' He glanced at his watch. 'Well, good luck then.'

As he walked away, Reuben began to load boxes of explosives into the heli.

'Demolition charges?' I said.

Reuben didn't even turn his head. 'You fly the helicopter,' he said. 'We'll take care of the rest.'

IT WAS DUSK before we took off and I made the customary transition to night-vision goggles for the flight. For once there was little gunfire to greet us as I flew in towards Bohara. It was as if, secure in their impending victory, the rebels had pulled back to recuperate before the final assault.

Rudi supervised the unloading of the demolition charges. They were at once fitted into backpacks and Raz, Reuben and Hendrik, their faces obscured with cam cream, slipped out of the gate and disappeared into the darkness, moving towards the mine workings.

Rudi spat in the dust. 'Waste of good plant,' he said. 'The Kaffirs couldn't use it anyway.'

I turned and walked away from him into the container building. I searched both tiers from one end to the other, then walked right around the compound. There was no sign of Layla.

I began stopping everyone I passed. 'Where's Layla?' I asked. 'Where's Layla?' All shook their heads or shrugged. I reached the main gate. 'Where's Layla?' I said to the guard.

'She went out an hour before dusk,' he said. 'She insisted she had some medicines for a patient in the workers' compound and wouldn't take no for an answer.'

'Was there a boy with her, an African kid?'

'Yeah.'

I knew at once where she had gone.

I returned to the building sick at heart. Rudi was sitting at a table, cleaning his fingernails with the point of a knife.

'Layla's missing,' I said.

He shrugged. 'So?'

'I have to find her.'

He laughed. 'When you've done the job you're paid for then you can go walkabout in the bush, crybaby. Right now, we've enough to do without worrying about some coloured bitch who's gone native.'

I looked away, waiting until I had controlled my anger. 'How soon do we leave?'

'The first group will go as soon as the demolition teams are back.'

'And the rest?'

'We'll hold the fort until you come back for us.'

We sat in silence for an hour until the demolition teams returned. Rudi selected eight men and sent them out to the heli. With all their kit, it was once more going to be dangerously overloaded.

'There's one more passenger,' Rudi said.

As I began to protest, I saw two men running from the container building, carrying a burden between them.

Grizz's corpse had been flexicuffed at the wrists and ankles to make it easier for them to carry. They ran stooping with it to the heli and tossed it inside without ceremony. Hendrik returned a final time with the severed head wrapped in a piece of sacking. He threw it onto the floor of the cab and I saw one of the mercenaries push it under the seat with the toe of his boot.

Only Rudi, Raz, Reuben and Hendrik now remained to hold the compound. 'Make sure you're back to lift us before dawn,' Rudi said.

I held out my hand. 'The diamonds.'

'Oh no. The diamonds stay here. If we let you fly out of here with them, what guarantee do we have that you'll come back for us?'

'I don't give a shit about the diamonds,' I said. 'All I want to do is get everybody out alive.'

'I'm touched by your concern, but perhaps Decisive Measures might have other priorities. This way we have an insurance policy.'

I fired up the helicopter and took off into the night. Somewhere in the blackness below me was Layla, if she was still alive.

As soon as we landed back at the airport, Colonel Pleydell and the Decisive Measures quartermaster strode out to meet us. The colonel was immediately surrounded by the mercenaries, airing the traditional soldiers' grievances about pay. While they argued, I shouted for a body bag. The quartermaster sauntered to a bunker and came back with a black rubber bag. I spread it out on the ground. 'Help me carry him out of the cab,' I said.

We lifted Grizz's body and laid it down on the rubber. 'We need to cut the flexicuffs off him,' I said.

'It doesn't matter to him.'

'It does to me. Just do it.'

He shrugged and cut off the flexicuffs with a knife.

I climbed back into the cab and pulled out the head from under the seat. I unwrapped it from the sacking, but could not bring myself to look at the face as I tried to arrange it in the body bag to give it some semblance of dignity.

'Make sure anyone who handles that shows some respect,' I said.

The quartermaster nodded. We lifted the bag onto the back of his Jeep and he drove across the airfield towards a waiting charter jet.

The colonel brushed the angry mercenaries aside and pushed his way through to me. 'You have the diamonds?'

'They're coming on the next trip.'

His thin, bloodless lips tightened. 'Those were not your orders.'

'I know that. Rudi and his mates back there weren't too eager about the original arrangement.'

He made a visible effort to control his anger. 'How soon can you be airborne again?'

'As soon as I'm refuelled.'

He turned away and started barking orders at the ground crew. They responded with sullen indifference and it was a good forty minutes before the fuel bowser had been brought out to fill up the tanks.

There was an understandable lack of enthusiasm among the mercenaries for one of them to act as a door gunner for the final mission to Bohara. The colonel tried bluster, cajolery and bribery in turn.

The plan that had been forming in my mind crystallised while I listened to the arguments. 'Don't sweat it, Colonel,' I said. 'I've managed without a copilot for the last few missions. I'm sure I can fly this one without a door gunner.' I settled the matter by turning away and pulling on my helmet as I hurried towards the cab.

I checked in with the tower, then I was airborne in a cloud of dust, banking southeast, back towards Bohara. Assuming I made it there, what happened after would depend entirely on Rudi, but I was pretty confident that I had his measure.

I switched on the night-vision goggles at 2,000 feet, allowing time for my eyes to become accustomed to the green-tinged, negative vision of the world below me before I began the descent.

I maintained radio silence until I was only a few miles from Bohara, then jabbed the radio button. 'Bohara, this is Grizzly One. Time for the last bus home. Give me a little light there, will you?'

Rudi's guttural Afrikaaner tones came at once through the static. 'Stand by. We'll light you in. There'll be a little diversion too.'

I saw the specks of green light flare in the distance as they began the prearranged signal: two long flashes, one short, three long.

As I slowed, preparing to land, the darkness beyond the base was lit by a series of blinding flashes as the demolition charges on the mine equipment erupted in succession.

A moment later the first ground fire cracked around me. I jinked and dodged, keeping the Huey moving around. The compound loomed ahead of me and I landed close to the container building.

Heavy weapon rounds were crashing down around the compound and the incoming fire redoubled as the remnants of the garrison—Raz, Reuben and Hendrik—sprinted for the cab.

Rudi was the last to leave the building. He sprinted low to the ground, clutching his rifle in his right hand and a chained steel case the size of a small cash box in his left. He dived through the door of the cab, yelling 'Go! Go! Go!'

I rammed up the collective and the Huey was airborne again. Torrents of tracer fire ripped through the night around us.

We were a bare 300 feet above the compound when the container building detonated. Flames climbed halfway towards the Huey.

The lack of return fire from the base must have told the rebels the last of the garrison had gone, and the ground fire ceased all at once, as if it had been switched off. I imagined them running through the darkness, tearing down the gates to loot whatever was left.

'Next stop R 'n' R,' Rudi said.

'Come up front a minute,' I said. 'I want to talk to you.'

'What about?'

'I'll tell you when you're up front.'

He pushed his way through the gap between the seats and slumped into the copilot's seat.

'Put the helmet on,' I said.

He gave me a suspicious look, but picked it up from the floor of the cockpit and pulled it onto his head.

'It keeps it private,' I said. 'Just between us. I've got a proposal.'

'And what do you propose?'

'A deal,' I said. 'I need your help to reach Layla.'

'You don't even know where she is.'

'I do know that. She's at Boroyende. I want you to help me find her and bring her and everyone else there to safety.'

He laughed. 'What have you got that could interest me?'

'Nothing much. Only ten million pounds' worth of diamonds. Colonel Pleydell is waiting to collect them at Freetown Airport. But we're here, while he's hundreds of miles away. So stuff him,' I said. 'You guys can split them between you. I'll ditch the heli and say we got shot down, the rebels got the diamonds and as far as I know they got you, too. You'll be posted missing in action. Just one of those diamonds'll buy you a new identity and a one-way ticket to a new life anywhere in the world.'

'Aren't you overlooking one thing? I have the diamonds, not you.'

'Sure you do, but at the moment we're at two thousand feet and heading for Freetown. When we land there, Decisive Measures and their friends will share the spoils and you will be left with a few thousand dollars in back pay and bonuses . . .'

I shot a quick glance at him and could see the predatory glint of his eyes in the darkness. I smiled to myself; I had him. 'All you've got to do is persuade the other guys to come with us,' I said.

'You're overlooking something,' Rudi said. 'What's to stop us taking off with the diamonds anyway, and leaving Layla and her Kaffir friends to rot?'

'Nothing, except if I set you down here, it'll take you three weeks to walk out . . . if you make it. But do as I ask and I'll drop you anywhere you want. We've got the range to go to Guinea, the Ivory Coast, even Senegal. We've plenty of fuel, I made sure of that.'

He sat in silence for some time, thinking it over. 'OK. You've got yourself a deal. But we'll keep it between ourselves for now. As far as the other guys go, this is part of the mission. OK?'

'OK,' I said. 'As long as you're sure you can persuade them.'

'I don't have to,' he said. 'They're soldiers, they take orders, and I outrank all of them.'

I gave an anxious look towards the eastern horizon. The first hints of dawn were already beginning to appear in the sky.

I switched my gaze back to the steep rocky ridge ahead of us, scouring it for the notch in the skyline that I was seeking—the landslip I had spotted some days before. Then I saw it a few miles ahead.

The instant that the ridge line cleared beneath me, I flared the heli and set it down in the notch in the hillside. Screened on either side and hidden from below by the lip of the landslip, it was invisible except from the air.

I shut down. Rudi was already climbing through to the cab. 'One more patrol, guys,' he said. There was a chorus of groans and argument, then Rudi's guttural voice rose, cutting through the dissent.

'I don't like it any more than you do, but those are the orders. We just get in and out; we get the job done, then we go home. And there's a bonus in it,' he said. 'Ten thousand dollars a head if we bring the coloured nurse out alive. She has some powerful friends.'

As they began to clamber down from the cab, I jumped down myself. Reuben and Hendrik helped me drag a camouflage net from the cab and drape it over the heli. I took particular care to obscure the Perspex canopy, covering it with branches and showering it with handfuls of dust to prevent it shining like a searchlight when the sun's rays struck it.

I glanced around. Rudi was standing off to one side, the case of diamonds still clutched in his left hand. 'Let's get moving,' he said. 'We need to be off this mountain before the sun gets much higher.'

I walked over to him and lowered my voice. 'Just one more thing first,' I said. 'We leave those diamonds here.'

He gave a brief humourless laugh, stuffed the case into the bottom pocket of his combat trousers, fastened the chain round his ankle and snapped the lock shut. He held the key in his closed fist for a moment, then turned and hurled it outwards, over the lip of the landslip. It glittered as it caught the light, then dropped from sight, tumbling down somewhere into the scree below us.

I shrugged and turned away. We formed a column and moved out, bathed in the strengthening light of dawn. Rudi and Raz led the way with Hendrik and Reuben bringing up the rear. I had the novice's position in the centre of the column, the safest place if we were ambushed and the one from where I could also put the others in the least danger through my inexperience.

Rudi paused for several minutes at the lip of the landslip, scanning the scree-strewn hillside below us, then led us out of the shade into the warmth of the rising sun. We moved along the slope for half a mile until we reached a dry stream bed. Then, half hidden by the cover of the jumble of rocks in the stream bed, we began to descend towards the distant line of the forest at the foot of the slopes.

The gradient eased as we descended. We passed the first stunted bushes and trees on the scree slopes, and we moved more slowly and cautiously as we neared the tree line. We paused on the edge of the forest to give our eyes time to adjust to the dim light under the tree canopy. Then we began to advance through the trees.

Birds and the occasional monkey moved through the roof of the forest high above us and butterflies fluttered through the pools of light where a fallen tree had pierced the canopy and allowed the sun to break through. Insects whined around my ears, feeding hungrily on any exposed flesh. We advanced slowly in total silence, communicating by hand signals. We paused every few yards to watch and listen, and check the GPS.

Boroyende lay no more than fifteen miles ahead of us, yet it would take us at least the rest of the day to reach it.

I could scarcely believe my recklessness in placing my trust in Rudi, but I could see no way that I could have made it through the forest and back without the help of his mercenaries. For all their brutality, these men were trained and experienced jungle fighters.

The fact that Rudi had lied to the others also concerned me. If he was planning some double-cross, he would certainly not want any witnesses to it.

As the slope grew more gradual, the ground became wetter and wetter. We crossed sluggish streams and waded through the first shallow ponds. Then, over the forest floor ahead of us, I saw the beginnings of a swamp. There was no way round it, for it spread for miles across the valley. We just had to go through it.

CHAPTER 12

We were still two miles short of Boroyende as night began to fall. We huddled together, thigh-deep in swamp water, as we discussed in whispers our next move.

'It's only two miles,' I said. 'Can't we just keep going?'

Rudi turned a scornful look on me. 'Have you ever tried to move through jungle at night? It's as black as your hat. All you would do is alert every rebel for miles around by the noise you made blundering through the undergrowth and scaring the wildlife.' He shook his head. 'We find some dry ground and bivouac there till morning.'

I knew he was right, but the thought of spending another night so near and yet so far away from Layla tore at my heart.

We stopped at a low hillock rising above the surface of the swamp. Rudi and the others had hammocks, brew kits and survival rations in their backpacks. I had almost nothing.

As dark fell we ate some rehydrated rations and drank a mug of tea, then Rudi ordered Raz and Reuben to keep guard as he and Hendrik settled into their hammocks slung between the trees. I curled up on the ground.

The swamp was alive with the noise of frogs and insects, and mosquitoes fogged the air around me. I barely slept and it was a relief to see the light filtering through the forest canopy as dawn broke.

We ate a frugal breakfast, brewed up some tea, and then moved out again on the trek over the last two miles to the village. After a mile we met rising ground and emerged at last from the dank waters of the swamp into the leaf litter of the forest floor.

The trees began to thin almost at once. As we reached the cultivated land, garden plots slashed and burned from the forest, we advanced slowly and stopped at the tree line. The village appeared utterly deserted, not even a scrawny chicken rooting in the dust.

The mercenaries worked their way through the village, covering each other as they cleared each hut. I followed them, the sense of foreboding growing inside me with each step. I peered into the village carpenter's hut. The neat rows of carefully polished tools had disappeared and the beautiful rocking chair lay in bits.

I moved on to Njama's hut. There were stains of dried blood in the dust just inside the doorway. The interior of the hut had been wrecked and the storage jars and plates had disappeared.

I looked up at the ceiling. The light bulb still hung there, but the glass had been shattered, leaving only a dangling bent and broken filament. It was a similar tale of destruction in every hut in the village; there was no sign of the occupants.

As I came out of the last hut, I saw Rudi and the other mercenaries standing just beyond the edge of the village, staring down into something at their feet. A feeling of dread overwhelmed me.

A crude pit had been dug in the ground where a mound now rose from it, covered in something black that seemed to move and shimmer as I looked at it. As I reached the edge of the pit, Rudi stretched out his rifle and prodded the mound. The black shimmering curtain rose into the air, a cloud of flies lifting to reveal the corpses beneath.

I found myself staring into the dead face of one of Njama's sons. Before I knew what I was doing, I had climbed down into the pit and begun to tear at the bodies, pushing them and dragging them aside, barely aware of the terrible stench of decaying flesh.

Three of Njama's four sons were dead. I dragged their bodies aside in turn and searched through the rest, finding old men and women, children and even babies buried there.

I crawled out of the pit, walked away from the others and stood alone, staring into the forest. I shook my head. 'There's no sign of Layla or Njama or Kaba here.'

'That doesn't mean they're alive. The rebels could have killed them somewhere else, or taken them away with them.' Rudi paused, studying my face. 'They'd certainly have wanted to have their fun with Layla before they killed her.' He was almost laughing at me.

My fists clenched, but this wasn't the moment to fight him. 'They could still be alive. We have to search for them.'

'How? Where? Even if they are alive, they could be anywhere.'

'They won't have strayed far from the village. We could light a signal fire, or fire a shot.'

'Don't be stupid. The only people that would bring running would be the rebels. Now I've kept my part of the bargain, it's time for you to keep yours.'

I thought of Layla lost in the forest around us. I threw back my head and cried out her name. I heard the scrape of steel on steel.

Rudi's rifle was pointing towards me and the safety catch was off. 'You do that again,' he said, 'and I'll leave you in the pit. Now'—he wrinkled his nose as he stepped closer to me—'get down to the river and wash or the rebels will be able to track us from the stench of dead meat and the trail of flies following us.'

I walked down to the river bank, sluiced the stench of death from me with river water and turned to walk back towards the village.

As I did so, I glimpsed a face peering at me from the undergrowth. I froze. Then the leaves parted and Kaba walked into the open. His hair was matted and his ribs showed through his skin but his face broke into a grin at the sight of me. 'You have come for us,' he said.

'Layla?' I hardly dared ask the question.

'She is safe.'

Relief washed over me. 'How many others?'

'Twelve.' The population of the village had been at least eighty.

'Where are they?' I said.

'In hiding a little way from here. I will take you to them.'

'Wait,' I said. 'We must bring the soldiers with us.'

I led him back into the village. His expression darkened when he saw Rudi. 'Why is he here?'

'He's here to help you—to help us all.'

'They're still alive,' I said to Rudi. 'They're near by. We must go and get them.'

His expression was unreadable. He studied me for a long time in silence. Then he shrugged his shoulders. 'Let's get on with it.'

The boy led the way down to the river, stepped into the current and began to wade upstream through the chest-deep water. We followed, holding our rifles above our heads. The river narrowed as it curved away out of sight. Both banks were smothered in vegetation, and branches and lianas hung down over the water, forming a tunnel through which we moved. It was as dark as dusk under the dense vegetation, but ahead I could see the glow of daylight.

We were approaching a sweeping bend in the river. Silt and sand had formed a small beach ending in a sheer rock face. The beach was only a dozen yards wide and at either end it was screened by a curtain of tree branches and lianas.

I glanced upstream and down. The curve of the river hid the beach from sight; the only way to come upon it was to wade the river as we had done or to fight our way through the jungle down to the bank opposite.

Kaba called softly from the shallows, then moved up onto the beach. I saw the foliage stir at the far end and an old woman stepped into the open. She gave an uncertain look from the boy to the semicircle of mercenaries flanking him, then she saw my face. She smiled, turned and said something to the people still hidden behind her.

Then Layla stepped into view. A moment later she was in my arms. I pulled her close and kissed her. She stiffened for a second, then leaned into me, holding my face in her hands, staring into my eyes. 'I'd given you up,' she said. 'I'm sorry that I doubted you.'

'You were right to doubt me,' I said.

She glanced over my shoulder at Rudi and the others. 'But why are they here?' she said. 'Don't tell me they've suddenly discovered a conscience.'

'It's strictly business for them. I bribed Rudi: diamonds for lives.' When I released her and looked up, I saw that the other survivors from the village had also emerged from hiding. There were two small children, a girl, a couple of teenage boys, and a number of older women. Njama was the last to emerge, leaning heavily on the shoulders of two of the women. There were dressings over wounds in his stomach, chest and arm, and his face bore the ravages of pain and grief, but he managed a flicker of a smile as he saw me.

I turned back to Layla. 'Is he fit to travel?'

'Not really, but if he stays here he'll die.'

Rudi took my arm and pulled me to one side. 'If we try to take the old man, we put all our lives at risk.'

'Just the same, he comes with us. I'm not leaving him to die.'

He stared at me in silence, then turned away. 'Come on.'

I lifted Njama onto my shoulders, waded out into the river and followed Rudi and the others back downstream. When we reached the village, I lowered Njama to the ground. Kaba and I helped him as he hobbled up the track and into the village.

Rudi led the way straight through and disappeared into the forest on the far side. As we made to follow him, Njama stopped us. He took a last look at what had once been his village. His eyes filled with tears as he turned his back and walked with us into the forest.

The four mercenaries spaced themselves through our ragged column with Rudi at the head and Hendrik bringing up the rear. We were very vulnerable to attack, however, strung out over forty yards in forest where the visibility was no more than five or six.

We made painfully slow progress at first, working our way through the dense vegetation, but after a while we found an animal track made by pigs or brush deer.

At my insistence, we stopped for a few minutes every hour. As soon as we did so, Njama sank to the ground and closed his eyes, his face grey. Each time, Layla examined him and checked his dressings; the wound in his stomach was beginning to weep again.

She met my gaze. 'He needs to rest.'

'We can't stop yet; we've too far to go.'

She bit her lip. 'All right, but not much further, then he must rest.'

The old man's frail voice cut through our discussion. 'I will make it,' he said. 'I will not let you down.'

We began to wade through the murky water of the swamp. I was soon exhausted from the effort of half carrying, half dragging Njama along, and I could hear his rasping breath at each step.

We collapsed to the ground when we reached the low mound rising above the surface of the swamp, where we'd slept the previous night. Layla examined Njama again. 'He can't go any further without proper rest,' she said.

I looked upwards. The light filtering through the forest canopy was bright; the sun must still have been quite high in the afternoon sky. I hesitated, then nodded. 'That's it,' I said to Rudi. 'We'll have to stop here. Njama can't go any further until he's rested.'

Rudi glowered at me as the other mercenaries clustered around him. 'What is this?' Reuben said. 'A patrol or a picnic in the woods?'

Raz took up the grievance. 'What are we doing here?'

'We're following orders,' Rudi said. 'We have a job to do.'

'Nursemaiding Kaffirs?' Hendrik said. 'Since when has Decisive Measures been interested in that?'

They looked on the point of mutiny. 'Maybe we should level with them,' I said.

Rudi met my gaze with a ferocious scowl and pulled me to one side, out of earshot. 'Need-to-know basis,' he said. 'They don't.' The others gave us sullen stares and I could hear them muttering to each other as we settled down to rest and prepare for the night. Rudi posted Raz and Reuben as guards, keeping them apart, I thought, so that they would have no further chance to share their grievances.

We had little food between us, and though Raz and Reuben

shared some of their rations, albeit with ill grace, Rudi and Hendrik kept all theirs for themselves. I cut brushwood and made a crude bed for the old man, raised a few inches above the sodden earth. He lay down, closed his eyes and was asleep at once.

Layla sat by him, her face etched with concern. As night began to fall, we curled up together on the ground.

Layla studied me in the twilight. 'Why did you come back?'

'I finally realised that what you told me was true. You can't escape responsibility by sitting on the sidelines or looking the other way. You've got to take sides and get involved; otherwise you're no better than the rest of them.'

We fell into an exhausted sleep, our arms round each other, but we were awake again before first light. As the light strengthened, we began moving on through the water. Kaba and I supported Njama, carrying him through the deepest parts of the swamp.

A few hours later, we stopped to drink a mug of swamp water, strained through a gauze dressing, and eat a few grains of rice and a piece of dried fruit. When we set off again, Rudi changed the marching order, putting the two younger mercenaries, Raz and Reuben, at the front of the column and bringing up the rear himself with the more experienced Hendrik.

In the gloom under the dense vegetation we could see no more than five yards ahead or behind us. We had been wading in single file through the swamp for almost two hours, when there was a burst of gunfire from the forest behind us. We hurried forward.

Raz and Reuben had stopped dead at the head of the column. They dropped into firing positions at either side of the animal track we were following.

Raz jerked his head at me. 'Take them on ahead,' he said. 'We'll follow when we've cleared the danger.'

Layla took over my role of supporting the old man as I moved to the head of the column. As I had seen Rudi and the others do, I paused every few yards to watch and listen, and kept checking the GPS, trying to keep us on a direct bearing to the helicopter. I lost all track of time as I inched forward through the swamp, my nerves jangling at each noise—the plop of a frog splashing into the water, the faint rasp of a snake's belly as it slithered away through the undergrowth or the cries of birds in the canopy high above us.

At last I could see the land beginning to rise ahead of us. We had reached the end of the swamp. One by one we emerged out of the water onto dry ground.

There was brighter light ahead and we reached a natural clearing where a giant tree had collapsed, tearing a hole in the forest canopy. I hesitated, peering towards the shadows on the far side of the clearing. A track ran through the middle at right angles to our course. I stayed hidden in the undergrowth, looking and listening.

Nothing moved and I heard no sound. After a couple of minutes, I waved the column forward, trying to cover them with the rifle as they crossed the clearing and disappeared back into the forest. Layla, Njama and Kaba had just begun to cross when I saw movement from up the track to my left. I shouted to them, 'Take cover! Fast!'

They dived into cover. I looked back to my left. A woman was walking slowly towards me. I stepped out into the centre of the track and held up my hand, palm out, to show her she had nothing to fear from us. Her face remained nervous, frightened.

That was nothing unusual; these were desperate times, when every stranger was to be feared, but something made me look again. As I peered at her, I saw the black mouth of a rifle poking out from under her arm, and in the dust behind her I saw a double shadow—the woman herself and another figure crouching behind her. I swung up my rifle and shouted at the woman, 'Get out! Get out of the way!'

She gave me a terrified look, whimpering with fright, but she didn't move. I saw the mouth of the rifle swinging towards me and threw myself back into the cover of the undergrowth. There was the crack of a rifle and a bullet smashed through the vegetation a couple of feet from my head. I rolled sideways and then belly-crawled a few more feet. As I did so I heard another single shot, and then a burst of gunfire shredded the undergrowth where I had been hiding. I slid my rifle forward and raised my head a few inches to peer out through the fronds of a fern towards the clearing.

The woman lay sprawled in the track, apparently dead, a pool of blood slowly widening around her. She had outlived her usefulness to the rebel soldier. He was now moving towards where I had disappeared into the undergrowth. He walked erect, not even bothering to stoop, certain of his own invulnerability.

I took aim, then squeezed the trigger. The rifle was set on semi-automatic. The first couple of rounds ripped through his chest, hurling him backwards. The rest of the burst sprayed high and wide, but he was already dead, slumped over the body of the woman he had killed.

I waved the rest of the column through, urging them on, then I dropped back to the rear. We had gone no more than fifty yards when I heard the sound of pursuit.

I wormed my way into the undergrowth, my rifle pointing back along the track we had made. I heard the sound of people moving fast, crashing through the undergrowth after us. Easing off the safety catch, I squinted along the barrel, drawing a bead where the track disappeared from sight, aiming about three feet above the ground. A figure burst into the open. My finger was already tightening on the trigger when I recognised the burly figure in camouflage fatigues. Rudi had only Raz and Reuben with him.

I called 'Rudi!' and, not wanting to be shot by reflex, I waited until I saw recognition in his eyes before I stood up.

'I saw your handiwork back there on the track,' he said. 'Not bad. We might make a soldier of you yet.' He paused. 'But I didn't think you English gentlemen killed women.'

'I didn't,' I said. 'The gunman killed her.'

He smiled. 'I believe you, English. I believe you.'

'What happened to you?' I said. 'What was the shooting?'

'Rebels. A small group. They won't be troubling us again, but they may have been the advance guard of a larger group.'

'There are only three of you. What happened to Hendrik?'

'Hendrik is dead. The rebels shot him.'

Something in the way he said it made the hairs on the back of my neck stand on end. He pushed past me and began to walk off up the track we were following.

Raz was white-faced and I could see a muscle tugging insistently in Reuben's cheek, counterpointing the rapid blinking of his eyes.

'I'm sorry about your mate,' I said. 'Were either of you with him when it happened?'

Raz shook his head and turned away to follow Rudi. I stood staring at the ground, a growing chill in the pit of my stomach.

CHAPTER 13

We overtook the struggling column within fifty yards and pushed on together, finally leaving the swamps behind and beginning the long, slow ascent towards the mountain.

I moved up alongside Rudi as he scanned the open hillside beyond the last of the trees. There was no one in sight, nothing moving on the whole expanse of hillside but, hampered by Njama's wounds, I knew that we would be exposed in the open for at least two hours before we could reach the landslip where the helicopter was hidden.

Rudi took a last look around, then turned to me. 'You go on with the others,' he said. 'We'll loop the track and make sure we're not being followed. If they catch us in the open out there, they'll cut us to pieces.'

I had the feeling that his words concealed more than they revealed.

He stood for a moment and touched his pistol, his ration pack and the grenades attached to his webbing, as if he were carrying out a mental checklist. Then he turned and hurried away. He hissed an order to the other two and they followed him back into the forest.

The rest of us moved out of the trees and we laboured up the hillside, slipping and stumbling over the loose rock and scree.

Njama's head lolled on his shoulders and his mouth hung open. He was exhausted. I handed Layla the rifle and hoisted the old man onto my back. As I stumbled slowly upwards, my head pounded from dehydration. We were still creeping up the dry stream bed and had another fifty yards or so to go to reach the contour line that would take us round to the mouth of the landslip. Then there was an explosion from the forest behind us, a single blast, followed by a burst of gunfire. I urged the others on and redoubled my own efforts.

I climbed until I thought my lungs would burst, then set Njama down for a moment and turned to look back down the hillside.

Rudi was just beginning to climb the stream bed behind us. He was alone and climbing fast, never once turning to look behind him.

He overtook us just as we reached the landslip. 'Where are the others?' I said.

'We were followed. They threw a grenade. They killed Raz and Reuben. I shot those rebels, but there'll be others. We have to get out of here fast.'

I stared at him.

'What's up with you?' he said. 'Let's go. Let's go.'

I kept staring at him. There was a gap on his webbing where a grenade had been hanging when he'd gone back into the forest.

'I only heard one grenade and one gun firing, Rudi,' I said.

He looked down, following my gaze. When he raised his eyes again, there was a cold murderous look in his eye and I now found myself staring down the barrel of his rifle.

He studied me for a moment, chewing his lip as he pondered his options. Then he shrugged. 'Less people to share the diamonds with, Jack. That's all you need to worry about. Just fly this heli over the frontier, ditch it in the jungle near a city and we walk out with a few million in diamonds each.'

I shook my head. 'No way.'

'You don't have a choice, Kaffir-lover,' he said.

I glanced towards the others and he laughed at me. 'You think that coloured whore or those Kaffirs will help you? If it means saving their own necks, they'll stand there and watch you die.'

Just the same, he moved slightly, trying to keep them in his sight as he confronted me. Njama's son just stood there blank-faced, but I saw Kaba slink away from Rudi towards the rocks. I didn't blame him. I'd have run for it too, if I could.

'Kill me and you're trapped,' I said. 'You can't fly the helicopter.'

'I don't need it. You think in twenty years' Kaffir-killing I haven't learned how to survive in the bush?'

'Then you'd better go ahead and shoot me,' I said. 'Because I'm not going anywhere without these people.'

His jaw worked and I saw his knuckles whiten as he tightened his grip on the trigger. The crack of a rifle shot reverberated from the rock walls around me. A bullet smashed into my shoulder, hurling me to the ground. I tried to push myself upright, then collapsed again as my shattered shoulder gave way beneath me. I stared stupidly at the blood soaking my right sleeve.

I looked up. Rudi's mouth hung open in a silent scream of pain and rage. His head was tilted to one side, and his right arm hung at a strange angle. A dark stain was spreading over his fatigues. I saw his fingers spread and his hand fall limp at his side. The rifle dropped to the ground, its butt streaked with blood.

Rudi turned to face his assailant, but as he did so Kaba struck again, reaching up on tiptoe like a kid stretching for a sweet jar, except that in his hand he held a bloodstained panga. Rudi let out a bellow and aimed a punch at the boy's head with his one good arm, but Kaba ducked underneath it and swung the panga again at the back of Rudi's knees. His hamstrings snapped like guitar strings and he collapsed to the ground.

Rudi and I stared at each other, both sprawled in the dirt, as Kaba advanced and stood over Rudi, his face devoid of expression.

'Kaba! No!' I shouted, but it was too late. The panga was already rising again. He held it two-handed, high over his head for a moment, then brought it whistling down with all his force across Rudi's neck, hacking his head from his body.

Kaba stood motionless, his face impassive as he stared at the dead man. No one moved until Layla got to her feet, walked over to the boy and laid a hand on his arm. He started, but made no resistance as she gently eased the panga from his fingers, and turned him away from the dead body, cradling his head against her chest.

One of the old women led him away as Layla ran to my side. I stifled a yell of pain as her fingers probed the wound. 'It's badly broken,' she said. 'I'll tie off the bleeders and then I'll have to set it and strap it up. I'll give you some morphine. It's going to hurt.'

'No morphine,' I said. 'I've got to fly the heli.'

'With a broken shoulder? You can't.'

'I have to. And you'll have to help me.'

'But I can't fly a helicopter.'

'You can if I tell you how to. If we don't get out of here we'll die, Layla. Either the rebels will kill us, or we'll starve to death. Now patch up my shoulder so I don't bleed to death on the way back and then let's get out of here. But, Layla,' I held her gaze. 'No morphine. I need to be alert or we're all dead.'

'You can't imagine how painful this is going to be.'

'Just do it,' I said.

She gave me a twisted piece of cloth to bite on and then began to clean the wound, picking out fragments of bone and tying off the severed veins. I kept my eyes averted most of the time, but it hurt like hell and I felt waves of hot nausea sweeping over me.

She paused for a moment and our eyes met. She kissed my forehead. 'Hold on,' she said. 'This is the really painful bit. I have to move your arm to set the bone, then I'll strap it across your chest.'

She called to Kaba and one of the women. They knelt either side of me and held me down as Layla straddled my chest and took hold of my arm. Electric stabs of agonising pain shot through me. I heard the dry scrape of bone on bone. The pain built and built until I thought my head would explode. Then I blacked out.

When I came round, Layla was still crouching over me, watching my face. The worry lines etched into her forehead faded as my eyes flickered open and she gave a gentle smile. 'Are you all right?'

My shoulder throbbed with a dull ache. I glanced down. My right arm was strapped across my chest. 'I think so. Help me up.'

She and Kaba supported me as I struggled to my feet. The effort sent more hot waves of pain coursing through me and I had to steady myself against Layla and close my eyes until it subsided.

'It's too soon,' she said.

I shook my head. 'Help me get this net off the helicopter.'

We hauled at the camouflage net and I sent Kaba up to wipe the thick layer of dust off the canopy.

Layla and Kaba then helped Njama to climb into the cab and laid him on the floor. The other villagers clustered around him.

I led Kaba over to Rudi's body. 'We need that case he's carrying,' I said. 'Can you break the chain with the panga?'

He studied it for a moment, then nodded. 'I can get it for you.' He raised the panga above his head and brought it down. There were no sparks and no sound of metal on metal, just a noise that was now all too familiar to me—a dull, wet thud like an axe chopping sodden wood. I looked down. Rudi's left foot had been severed at the ankle. Kaba reached down and pulled the bloodied chain over the stump and offered me the case.

'Just put it in the cockpit of the helicopter,' I said. I turned to Layla. 'Let's get airborne. I can still do most of the work, but you'll have to operate the cyclic for me.'

She stared at me. 'This is madness. I can't help you fly this. We'll crash and be killed. We can walk out instead.'

I shook my head. 'We'd be dead long before we reached the frontier. How long would I or Njama last? Or the old women? Or you? Even Kaba would struggle to make it. It's the only way, Layla.

'I told you all this once before, remember? I can still operate the rudders, the throttle and the collective, all you've got to worry about is the cyclic. The controls are duplicated for the pilot and the copilot. All you have to do is move your cyclic when I tell you. The movements required are very small, absolutely minimal. If I see you do anything wrong, or feel, by the other controls, that you've overcooked it, I'll get you to correct it. We may fly like a drunk on a rollercoaster, but we will keep airborne. Trust me?'

She studied my face, then gave a slow, reluctant nod.

I smiled with a bravado I was far from feeling. 'Then let's do it, before either of us realises what fools we're being.'

Layla slid the cab door closed, then helped me up into the cockpit. I couldn't get my flight harness over my injured arm, so I remained unstrapped. She put on her own harness, then sat back in the seat as far as possible and closed her eyes.

I settled my feet on the rudder pedals and gripped the collective with my left hand. The pain in my shoulder had subsided a little, but it was still bad enough to make the sweat stand out on my brow, and any movement sent a fresh stab of pain searing through my body.

'Right,' I said. 'Get the feel of the cyclic before we do anything else.'

She opened her eyes and took hold of it in a tentative grip, her forearm resting across her thigh.

'You have to hold the cyclic more firmly than that,' I said. 'When we fire up the engines it'll start to shake around.'

She took a firmer grip on it.

'That's better,' I said. 'Now practise moving it around. Go left . . . right . . . forward . . . back . . . That's fine, except that you're moving it too far. Try again, but no more than a quarter-inch in any direction. Better to have to nudge it further than ram it over and then drag it back again.' I paused. 'Right, helmets on.'

She helped me fasten the strap under my chin, then fixed her own. I turned a little in my seat to look back into the crowded cab and it caused an agonising stab of pain to shoot down my arm. I gasped.

Layla shot me an anxious look. 'All right?'

I nodded. 'Let's get this thing airborne.' Reaching awkwardly across my body with my left hand, I stretched up and pushed the levers into ground idle. I waited until the fresh jolt of pain in my shoulder had subsided a little, then pressed the starter. There was an electric whine over our heads and the left engine began to turn over.

I stared at the RPM gauge, waiting for it to reach double figures, then pushed the fuel switch. The engine roared and I repeated the process for the right engine. When both were running, I checked the gauges and warning panels, then pushed the control into flight idle. I raised the collective gently until the heli lifted on its springs, poised to take flight. I looked at Layla. 'Don't worry. You'll do fine. Just don't panic and keep listening to what I'm telling you. Even if we seem to be out of control, we can pull it all back together as long as neither of us panics.'

I could see her hand shaking with the mechanical vibrations through the cyclic, and her knuckles whitened as she grasped it still more tightly.

'Now, our first problem is to get out of this landslip without touching the sides. If we can do that, the rest should be a doddle. All we'll have to worry about then is landing at Freetown. So, in a moment I'm going to raise the collective, and as I do so I want you to ease the cyclic forward a touch. Don't move it to either side, just forward. There's a fractional time-lag before the heli responds, so don't think it isn't working and give it some more, or we'll be heading down again rather quickly.'

I turned my head to call into the back. Even that slight movement caused another wave of pain. 'All right back there? Hold tight to the sides, we're taking off in a second and it's bound to be a rough flight.' I heard the frail voice of Njama translating what I had said.

'Right, this is it,' I said, and raised the collective. 'Cyclic forward a touch.' As the heli began to lift, sluggish under its heavy burden, Layla moved the control forward. She hesitated and then nudged it forward again. 'That's too much,' I said. 'Wait for the response.'

She corrected it, but the Huey clattered down again and bounced back into the air. Unrestrained by any harness, I was thrown up with it, and then crashed down again onto the seat, jerking the controls around in my hands. I bit my lip as a fresh burst of pain hit me.

The Huey was airborne again, but beginning to drift left. 'Ease it right a fraction,' I said.

'It's not responding.' Again she moved the cyclic further.

'Give it time,' I snapped. 'Move it left.' I saw the rock wall looming beyond her. 'Left now!'

She responded, but overcorrected and we began to drift towards the left-hand rock face. 'Forward,' I said, raising the collective again. The engine note and the beat of the rotors picked up, but we were now both dipping towards the rocky floor of the landslip and drifting dangerously close to its wall. 'Now back and right again. Right!'

We lurched away from the rocks and shot up into the air. I raised the collective to stop us from stalling, but Layla was already making a semi-instinctive correction, pushing the cyclic forward again. We hurtled down, caught the lip of the landslip with a thud that sent us bouncing back high into the air. The disc of the rotors scythed through the air by the right-hand rock wall, shredding the parched shrubs clinging to its face.

'Left, left!' I shouted. 'Forward!'

I raised the collective again and we lurched out of the mouth of the landslip. I heard Layla's indrawn breath as she saw the land falling away below us. 'It's all right,' I said. 'You're doing great.'

I risked a glance at her. Through the Perspex of her visor I could see her hair matted with sweat against her forehead. 'Now we need to pick up some speed,' I said, 'and climb to clear the ridge. Just hold it steady and give it a little forward nudge.'

This time I waited a fraction of a second before raising the collective, realising—not before time—that it was easier for me to adjust to her movement of the cyclic than the other way round.

As I moved the controls, even above the thunder of the rotors, I heard the crack of gunfire. I looked down. 'Shit!' I said. 'Rebels.' The mountainside below us was black with soldiers. Bullets chipped fragments from the rocks around the mouth of the landslip and a moment later there was a whoosh, a crash and a starburst of smoke and flame as a round from an RPG streaked inches past the Huey.

'Climb!' I shouted. 'Back and left on the cyclic. Back and left!'

I yanked the collective upwards, twisting the throttle viciously as I stamped on the rudder pedal, swinging us round to face the cliff. There were cries and groans from the cab as the villagers were thrown around by the manoeuvre.

Rounds continued to clang against the armoured underside of the heli. If the soldier with the RPG got his next shot on target, it would pierce the armour as if it were paper and blast us out of the sky.

We had to put the ridge line between us and the rebel gunner before he could get off another shot, but an even more immediate danger was now threatening us. Taking me at my word, Layla had made the most minimal movement of the cyclic. It was not enough. The rock face just below the ridge loomed in front of the cockpit, filling my vision. 'Back on the cyclic! Back! Back! Give it more!'

Slowly, ponderously, the Huey responded and the nose began to come up. Weighed down by the people in the cab, the engines were screaming as they strained to deliver the power I was demanding through the controls.

Although we were climbing slowly, the ridge line was rushing to meet us. Blue sky showed in the top half of the canopy, but the rest of my vision was filled with black, unforgiving rock. 'We're not going to make it,' I yelled, trying to brace myself for the impact.

There was a crash and a sickening lurch as the skids hit the rock just below the summit. More cries came from the back and I almost passed out with pain. As the heli tipped forward, and even before I had time to speak, Layla had begun to correct, forcing the cyclic back to counter the dip of the nose.

There was another crash and a terrible scraping, gouging sound as the skids bit into the solid rock. The turbines climbed the octaves, shrieking at the strain imposed on them, then the Huey spun to the right and its momentum threw it clear.

At once we were climbing almost vertically, still with the sound of bullets smacking against the metal skin of the heli. The screaming engines faltered at stalling point. 'Forward, now!' I said.

The engines picked up again and we began to level, but rounds were still puncturing the fuselage. 'Forward again. More.'

The sounds of gunfire faded and stopped as we plummeted down the far side of the ridge, out of sight of our pursuers. I fought for control of the Huey and, as soon as we levelled, I piled on the power again, putting as much distance as possible between us and the ridge line before any rebel soldiers reached it.

I glanced at Layla. 'You were fantastic,' I said, as soon as I had got my breath back. 'A natural pilot. Now let's get out of here.'

CHAPTER 14

We flew on into the west. Layla tried hard to hold the Huey in straight and level flight, but we still kept drifting from side to side as she corrected, recorrected and overcorrected the cyclic.

'It's got a mind of its own,' she said.

I could hear the tremor of fear in her voice. 'You're doing great.'

After a few more minutes she was able to hold it within a five degree arc of the direction I wanted us to be facing. We made slow progress, like a ship tacking into the wind, but with every minute we were cutting the distance separating us from Freetown.

I got Layla to push the radio button and spoke to the tower at the airport. 'Mayday. Mayday. Mayday. This is Grizzly One. Pilot wounded, helicopter overloaded, request immediate clearance to land. I repeat, immediate clearance. Over.'

A voice cut through the hiss of static. 'Grizzly One, this is Freetown tower. We have operational military traffic flying from here in support of a ground offensive. Request you divert to Conakry.'

'Negative, tower. I have insufficient fuel and we're close to falling out of the sky and so overloaded we can't even hover. We're coming in from the east, repeat east, and we'll need a clear runway to set down. ETA five minutes. Over and out.'

The radio squawked again at once, but I ignored it. 'Here comes the tricky bit,' I said to Layla.

Almost as soon as the words were out of my mouth, I saw streaks of red and orange tracer stabbing up into the sky. 'We've got to keep moving,' I said. 'And not offer a predictable target.'

'You mean keep flying it the way I have been?' she said. It was a brave attempt at a joke, but her voice cracked as she made it.

We were at 2,000 feet, a questionable range for an assault rifle, but well within range of anything heavier. The tracer bursts kept coming, lines of fire bright enough to show even against the afternoon sun. They began to get our range and the wavering lines cut through the sky towards us.

'Push it right and forward.' As I spoke, I hit the right rudder pedal and dumped the collective. The force of the diving turn pinned me against the side of the cockpit. I couldn't stifle a yell of pain. 'Sorry,' I said. 'But I'm all right, really. Now take it left and pull back.'

I waited until I saw her hand start to move, then raised the collective. Each manoeuvre was greeted by a chorus of screams and cries from the back, for few of the villagers had any handholds and they toppled and slid from side to side as we threw the heli around.

As we continued the evasion, Layla moved the cyclic to send us lurching upwards and downwards, and drifting from side to side in a way that even I could not predict. 'If they hit us it'll be sheer fluke,' I said. 'No gunner in the world could track this pattern.'

If it was hubris, it got the punishment it deserved. A few seconds later, the orange fires of bursting flak flared up across our track. I stamped on the rudder and shouted an order to Layla, but even as she moved the cyclic I heard the tinny rattle of shrapnel against the fuselage and then a crack from the tail boom.

I felt the tail of the heli begin to swing left. The tail rotor countered the torque from the main rotor. If it was damaged, the torque would force the body of the heli around. If it had been destroyed altogether, the heli would gyrate around its own axis until it hit the ground or tore itself apart.

I stamped on the right rudder, trying to counter the swing of the fuselage. There was a heart-stopping pause before I felt it begin to slow. We began to make forward progress again, but if I relaxed the pressure on the rudder it immediately began to spin.

My calf muscles were beginning to ache from the effort of holding down the rudder pedal, and I found it hard to concentrate on what Layla was doing with the cyclic. Our flight became ever more erratic, the Huey staggering across the sky like a drunk.

There was another burst of flak, another rattle as shrapnel knifed into the fuselage and then the clamour of a warning siren.

We had to contend with the smoky, choking stench of burning oil as the pressure gauge on the right engine registered a drop. Almost at once I heard it choking and banging. The altimeter began to unwind in jerks, dropping a few feet, levelling as the engine caught and fired smoothly again, then dropping once more as it spluttered and almost died.

I stared straight ahead, ignoring the flak, willing the heli on towards the airport, now clearly visible ahead.

I called the tower once more. 'Mayday. Mayday. Mayday. Tower, this is Grizzly One. Now losing oil, engine failure imminent. Please clear the airfield and prepare for crash landing. Over.'

The flak faded away behind the heli and I saw below us the front line of the fighting. Nigerian armour was rolling along the airport road towards Freetown.

Now safe from ground fire, I was torn between the need to keep enough altitude to reach the airport and the knowledge that if the engines failed at this height no autorotative landing on earth would save us.

The heli steadied, rose a little and then dipped again. We lurched from side to side as Layla tried to correct with the cyclic. Fresh waves of hot pain jabbed through me as I was thrown around in my seat.

The airfield perimeter was now less than a mile ahead, but the oil-pressure gauge had ceased to register, the engine was banging and clanking, belching filthy black smoke, and the smell of burning and hot metal was almost overpowering.

The effort of forcing down the rudder pedal was making my leg shake and tremble. I let the pressure slip for a fraction of a second and the heli at once slewed sideways. I gritted my teeth and stamped down again, counting silently to myself as I tried to hold it down and faintness and nausea once more threatened to overwhelm me.

I heard Layla's voice from a long way off. 'Hold on, Jack, we're almost there. Hold on.'

We were fifty yards from the perimeter fence when the right engine exploded into flame. The heli gave a sickening lurch. 'Cyclic left. Left!' I shouted as we slid sideways and downwards.

Layla jerked it too far and we began to slip the other way. The perimeter fence loomed ahead of us. The drop had at least allowed a microsecond for the revs to build in the remaining engine. I squeezed another couple of feet of altitude from the feeble increase in power. Smoke began to fill the cockpit and the heat from the burning engine overhead was fearsome. If we didn't get it down in the next few seconds we might be blown apart in midair.

We had reached the fence. The heli jerked and almost stalled as it snagged the wire, then began to topple sideways. Spontaneously, I released the rudder pedal and kicked down hard on the opposite rudder. Driven by the torque, the tail boom whipped round. The force catapulted us clear of the fence, but the heli smashed down on its right-hand side, shattering the flailing rotors like toothpicks.

I howled in agony as I was thrown across the cockpit and landed full on my fractured shoulder, on top of Layla. As the wave of pain ebbed away, I shouted 'Out! Out! Out! Jump for your lives!'

Black smoke swirled around us, and even through the visor of my helmet I felt the searing heat of the blazing engine. The steel case containing the diamonds had been crushed by the impact. Its twisted lid lay ajar and half a dozen diamonds glittered in the dust of the cockpit floor. I began scrabbling for them.

'Stuff the diamonds,' Layla said. 'Leave them.'

'You get out, I'm right behind you,' I said. 'Run. Get away from the heli.'

As she dropped from sight down the side of the cockpit, the heli burst into flames. With the fire spreading and dense smoke filling the body of the Huey, the bruised and battered villagers scrambled for the cab door. They began to tumble out of it, falling the few feet to the concrete and crawling away from the heli.

Coughing and choking, I fumbled with the steel case, then pushed at the cockpit door. It was stuck fast. Above the roar of the flames licking around the fuselage, I could hear Layla screaming for me to get out. I lay on my back, barely able to breathe for the stinking clouds of smoke enveloping me, and kicked out with my feet. There was a crack and an inrush of air as the door sagged open.

Still clutching the steel case in my good hand, I launched myself outwards and fell heavily to the ground. I lay there winded, my clothes smouldering, until Layla helped me to my feet.

'Did everyone get out?' I said.

She nodded. She helped me up and supported me, an arm round my waist, as I hobbled away from the stricken Huey. The villagers were strung out ahead of me in a ragged line across the concrete.

I heard the clamour of a fire truck, but before it could reach the heli, there was a bang like a sonic boom. We were blown forward, hurled into the dirt as the blast wave flashed over us and burning fragments rained down around us. I looked back. The Huey was a smoking ruin, a tangle of black, twisted metal. Layla helped me up and we moved on again to the dirt and parched grass at the edge of the airfield. Then I sank down, resting my head on my good arm.

Layla took my pulse and pulled off my helmet and laid a hand on my brow. Then she peeled back the dressing to examine my shoulder wound. 'It looks all right,' she said. 'Do you feel OK?'

'Never better.' I began to laugh at the stupidity of my remark, but it ended in a choking fit. 'My shoulder hurts like hell, of course, but thank God we all made it safely. You did a great job to get us here.'

'Are you sure you feel all right? Your speech is slurred again.'

'I'm fine. Just dog-tired.'

I put my hand to my mouth, then pressed it against my shoulder, wincing as if another spasm of pain had hit me.

She reapplied the dressing. Over her shoulder, I saw Colonel Pleydell marching over the concrete towards us, flanked by a posse from Decisive Measures.

I let my head sink onto my chest and half closed my eyes,

waiting until I saw the colonel's immaculately polished toecaps come to a halt in front of me before I raised my head again. 'Sorry about the Huey, Colonel,' I said. 'Hope it's insured.'

He stared at me for a moment. 'You left for Bohara three days ago. Where the hell have you been?'

'Engine trouble, Colonel. We were damn lucky I managed to patch it up enough to get back here at all.'

He gave me a dubious look, then waved his hand towards Njama and the others. 'Who the hell are all these people?'

'Human beings. Refugees.'

'Where are the others?'

'Rudi and the guys? They took off into the bush. Said they preferred to take their chances with the rebels than risk the flight back with me. Since I was coming back empty I took the opportunity of bringing these people with me.'

It took him a full minute before the implications of Rudi's disappearance hit him. 'Where are the diamonds?'

I handed him the steel case. He stared suspiciously at the battered lid, then knelt down, opened it and tipped out the diamonds to make a gleaming mound in the dust. He began counting them. When he straightened up again, his face was contorted with anger. 'There should have been seventy-four diamonds in this case. Six are missing.'

'Well, I haven't got any. Maybe they're still in the cockpit. You're welcome to go and search for them. Or talk to Rudi and those guys about it. They just handed me the case; I didn't ask how many were in it.' I paused as if the thought had just struck me. 'Maybe that's why they were so happy to risk it in the bush.'

He stared at me. 'Search him.'

His heavies manhandled me to my feet. I yelled in pain as one took my right arm.

'What are you doing?' Layla said. 'He has a serious wound and a fractured shoulder, and he's lost a lot of blood. Leave him alone and get him an ambulance.'

Pleydell swivelled to look at her. 'Who are you, pray?'

'I'm a paramedic with Medicaid International.'

He sneered at her. 'When I want advice from representatives of communist front organisations, I'll ask for it. This man is suspected of the theft of a number of diamonds and whether you like it or not, he will be searched.'

'It's OK, Layla,' I said. 'I'll be all right.'

The heavies looked to Pleydell for guidance. 'Get on with it,' he said. 'Search him.' Half-apologetically, one of them began to pat me down. 'Not like that,' Pleydell said. 'We're looking for diamonds not a pistol, for Christ's sake. Strip-search him.'

They stripped off my boots and trousers and searched every seam. Then they undid my shirt and body-searched me. They even began pulling back the bandages and peering at my wound, but I let out such a yell that they stopped at once. The sweat on my ashen face should have been enough to convince them that I was not faking.

'That's enough,' Layla said.

Pleydell gave me a long stare. Then a faint smile crossed his face. 'His mouth,' he said. 'Search his mouth.'

His men stared uncertainly from him to Layla.

Cursing, he pushed them aside. I obliged him by opening my mouth. He peered into it, and felt between my teeth and my cheeks with his finger. 'Lift your tongue,' he said.

'What?'

'Lift your tongue.'

I made a show of hesitation, then did as he asked.

He felt around under my tongue then stepped back, wiping his fingers on his trousers.

Pleydell still directed his baleful stare at me. 'Don't think for a moment this is over. I'll have more to say to you when we get back to England. The charter's waiting. I want you aboard inside ten minutes.'

'You don't understand, Colonel,' I said. I looked from him to Layla. Beyond her Njama and the other villagers sat silent and watchful. Layla stared back at me, holding my gaze with a look that told me all I needed to know.

I turned back to face Pleydell. 'I like it here. So as far as I'm concerned, you can stick your orders and your diamonds. I'm going nowhere, I'm staying here.'

Pleydell's mouth worked. 'To hell with you then. You're in breach of contract, and your wages are forfeit. See how long you last without money in this stink-hole of a country.'

He turned and marched away, followed by his men. As our ragged band made slow, shambling progress around the perimeter towards the airport buildings, I saw the Tristar's doors close. The engines fired and it taxied to the end of the runway. A couple of minutes later it took off towards the setting sun.

As the rumble of its engines faded, I turned to Layla. 'Could you change my dressing? Those diamonds are bloody uncomfortable.'

She stared at me for a moment and then began to laugh. She carefully peeled back the dressing and a few moments later she dropped six perfect, if bloodstained, diamonds into my hand.

I turned them over, watching the light shimmering through them, then passed them to Njama. 'These belong to you,' I said. 'You'll need them. Once the rebels are beaten, we've got a lot of rebuilding to do.'